TAKEN
TO THE
CLEANERS

OUT, OUT, DAMN SPOT . . .

My shoes crunched on the broken shards as I tried to move around the heavy piece of furniture toward the front door. The display case had fallen against it, pinning me inside. I changed directions. As I did, I kicked one of the statues and groped around on the floor to pick it up. Just in case.

I didn't think my attacker was here anymore, but one could never be too careful. I felt my way along the wall to where I'd seen the light filtering out from the other room and fumbled for a switch.

I flipped it on, and the statue slipped out of my hand.

There was no vandalism here. Just a man. Lying on the kitchen floor, wearing one of the freshly starched shirts we'd probably laundered and pressed for him just a few days before.

It was covered with blood.

TAKEN
TO THE
CLEANERS

Dolores Johnson

Dolores Johnson

A Dell Book

Published by
Dell Publishing
a division of
Bantam Doubleday Dell Publishing Group, Inc.
1540 Broadway
New York, New York 10036

ISBN: 1-56865-427-8

Printed in the United States of America

ACKNOWLEDGMENTS

I wish to acknowledge the assistance of the following people: Jim Nixon of Nu-Way Cleaners, Greeley, Colorado; Carolyn Varian of Bow Tie Cleaners in La Cañada, California; Larry Berman, Gigantic Cleaners and Gift Hanger, Aurora, Colorado; Norton Boslow, Gigantic Cleaners, Denver, Colorado; Father Michael Suchnicki of Samaritan House in Denver; Detective Michael Fiori of the Denver Police Department, and Stephen Cantrill, M.D. Any errors are mine and not the fault of the people who provided me with information.

In addition, I wish to thank the members of my Boulder critique group and the writers who assemble at Lee Karr's home for their advice and support. A special thanks to my agent, Meg Ruley, and her associate, Ruth Kagle.

To my son, Jeff,
who showed me that
dreams can come true
with perseverance and hard work.
Thanks for sharing dreams.

TAKEN
TO THE
CLEANERS

CHAPTER 1

Always wait on customers in order. That's a rule at Dyer's Cleaners, but I had to make an exception when Betty the Bag Lady showed up before eight o'clock Monday morning, pushing a shopping cart that wouldn't steer straight.

I tried to ignore her, but it was hard to do. She had trouble maneuvering the cart through the front door, letting in a blast of cold December air, and she nearly knocked over our Christmas tree. The rickety cart careened by several customers as Betty made her way to a gold-colored chair near the counter. It totally distracted the well-dressed woman I'd been waiting on.

"As I was saying," I repeated, "I'm Amanda Dyer, the owner."

My customer could have cared less. She had turned and was staring at Betty, who rustled like dry leaves as she settled herself in the chair. It sounded as if she were wearing taffeta instead of industrial-strength plastic.

Betty gives a whole new meaning to the term *bag lady*.

She's known as the Hefty Bag Lady around the neighborhood, but actually she only wears the heavy-duty plastic bags in the winter. In the summer she prefers to protect her clothes with the used garment bags from our plant. Uncle Chet had called it a form of recycling.

I'd inherited Betty along with the cleaners and a cat named Spot when my uncle died two years ago. I like to think I also inherited his sense of humor, but this was almost too much.

Uncle Chet used to buy an extra doughnut for the bag lady when he got them for his crew, and I'd continued the practice. As far as I knew, this was the first time she'd ever come around to the front of the plant looking for a handout.

"Hi, Princess," she said, waving at me.

At least, she hadn't called me Princess Di the way she usually did. The first time she'd addressed me that way, I'd been puzzled. I'm five foot five, have curly dark hair and couldn't have fit my size-12 figure into one of Diana's ball gowns with a shoe horn. In fact, the only things Diana and I have in common is that we're both thirtysomething and are recovering from failed marriages, although mine is without any heirs to the throne.

Betty had chortled at my bewilderment when she'd come up with the nickname and said not to let it go to my head. It was "Di" for Dyer, not Diana. I should have known better than to take the name as a compliment from a woman who considers a plastic bag a fashion statement.

But maybe Betty's way with words is why Uncle Chet had always looked out for her. After all, he'd called his original dry-cleaning plant Dyer's Cleaners and Dyers. It was like those old burlesque houses that advertised "40 Girls 40" on the marquee, or so he'd said.

He'd dropped the *and Dyers* from our sign when he built this fancy new plant near the Cherry Creek Mall and the Denver Country Club. Most cleaners don't do much dyeing of clothes anymore. However, somewhere in our family tree there must have been an English forefather who'd been a dyer and used the name of his trade for our surname.

That didn't mean all of us Dyers had inherited the gene for cleaning and dyeing. I'd worked for my uncle in his downtown store as I was growing up, but it hadn't been my first career choice. In fact I'd wanted to be an artist until my uncle died and left me this fancy new plant with a mortgage clear up to the steam vents on the roof. My husband, Larry, had just left me at the time, and I'd been so angry I'd locked myself in my studio apartment and painted dark, ugly slashes on canvases that I couldn't show to anyone. It just wasn't the way to support myself once the marriage collapsed, so becoming a dry cleaner began to look like a better and better option. I went back to my maiden name and tried to resurrect some long-dormant clean gene that must surely lie buried inside me.

While Betty jockeyed her shopping cart into position in front of her, I made an effort to regain my customer's attention. "Is this your first visit to our cleaners?"

The woman nodded her neatly coiffed blue hair, the type that white-haired women get when they go to a salon and have the dinginess chemically removed. She clutched her dirty clothes as if it might also be her last. The two other customers behind her in line also seemed intrigued by the bag lady.

Betty, on the other hand, was looking innocently around the call office, which is what we cleaners call the front end of the plant. Mine has an ultramodern design, all black and white, with lots of glass and stainless steel rails for the clothes, a mural on one wall, and several oil paintings on the other.

The bag lady seemed particularly interested in our up-and-down conveyor, which comes out of the back room through an opening in the wall and rises like a stairway to circle the ceiling overhead. Soon she had the other customers looking up at it, too, all except for the first-timer at the counter, who never took her eyes off Betty.

"I'll need your name, and if you'll give me your phone number, we'll use it as your account number," I said, accessing our computer, which is a state-of-the-art system Uncle Chet had installed when he'd relocated the cleaners from downtown Denver to this new plant that had been inspired by one he'd seen in California.

"I'm Mrs. William Adamson, and . . ." The woman's voice trailed off.

"Don't you know it ain't polite to stare?" Betty asked, glancing over to the counter and giving the woman a gap-toothed smile as if she were the only one who knew the first thing about good manners.

Mrs. Adamson sucked in her breath.

So much for my rule about taking customers in order. I went to the door into the cleaning plant and yelled at one of my employees, "Lucille, will you come out here and see what Betty wants?"

Lucille, who'd worked for my uncle for years, didn't like waiting on customers. She felt you could find out more about people from their clothes than you could from talking to them. For instance, she said lipstick on a man's collar meant he was playing around, and sexy lingerie from Victoria's Secret meant a woman was "hot to trot."

She came out of the back room, her smile as tight as the dishwater-blond curls on her head. She just didn't have the personality for the counter, and I tried to shield her from it whenever I could.

As soon as Betty saw her, the bag lady began to shake her head. "I need to talk to the Princess there."

"Okay." I knew when to admit defeat. "Lucille, why don't you help Mrs. Adamson and I'll take care of Betty?"

Lucille nodded, her curls not even moving. I always wondered how they stayed in place. Even though I kept my hair short, it was usually out of control, probably from all the steam in the back of the plant.

I brushed an errant lock out of my eyes and walked around the end of the counter to the chair.

"Thanks, Princess." Betty favored me with another smile as she rose to her feet, her plastic outerwear crackling like a bowl of Rice Krispies.

There was something about the bag lady's face that always fascinated me. Her hair, poking out from under a knit cap, was a yellowish-gray, not unlike Mrs. Adamson's would have been without the salon fix. Betty had black eyebrows and dark eyes that never seemed to miss a thing. Her weathered skin had wrinkles that sprayed out from her eyes and made a parenthesis around her mouth. They weren't tanned like the rest of her face, and they gave her a permanent smile, as if they were laugh lines etched into her skin in a happier time.

"I got something for you," she said.

"What do you mean?"

"It's something that belongs to you. I found it in a trash can up the street."

She lifted a paper sack out of her cart and opened it.

Inside was one of the yellow nylon bags we give out to delivery customers for their dirty clothes. I could see the Dyer's Cleaners logo on the side as she started to remove it from the sack, but I couldn't see the name tag that would have told me what customer it belonged to.

"I figured you'd want it back."

It was probably naive of me to think she'd decided to return it as a thank-you for all the doughnuts she'd eaten. I started to take it anyway.

She pulled it back. "There's something in it," she whispered loudly. "It's a fancy man's suit—worth a lot if I was to sell it."

Okay, so I was wrong. She wanted money, and she wasn't going to let me have it until I paid for it.

"It sure looks expensive," she said. "Must have been stolen from one of your customers."

I would reserve judgment on that until I'd seen it. Maybe it was worn out or torn so badly it couldn't be repaired.

"Can't figure why the fella would throw away a good suit like that—less it was stolen," she continued. "Five minutes later and the garbage truck woulda got it."

"I'll be right back." I went over to Lucille at the counter. "Would you give me twenty dollars out of the register?"

I returned and handed the bill to Betty. If the suit was worthless, I'd have to consider the money a charitable contribution, but I knew Uncle Chet would have disapproved. He'd once admitted doughnuts weren't the best diet in the world, but he said they were better than the booze she'd buy if he gave her money.

Betty lifted her shiny plastic outerwear and put the money in the recesses of her clothes. "Thanks, Princess. I knew you'd be glad to have it back." She handed the yellow bag to me and turned to leave.

Mrs. Adamson was in the process of doing the same thing, apparently having decided not to leave her clothes with a cleaner who would accept drop-off work from a bag lady. As the elegantly clad woman opened the front door, Betty wedged her cart in the opening, forcing Mrs. Adamson to act as doorperson.

"Now, that's what I call being polite," Betty said, winking at the other woman.

I tried to hide a smile as I went back behind the counter and opened the drawstring on the bag to check for the name tag that had to be stuck down inside.

Before I could find it, a man in a tan jogging suit stepped out of the other line and up to the counter across from me. "What was that all about, Mandy?" he asked.

I looked up at him as I fumbled inside the bag. "Oh, hi, David. You picking something up this morning?"

He nodded, but he couldn't seem to get over Betty. "Who was that old gal anyway?"

This time I couldn't help grinning. "Just a Good Samaritan who happens to believe in the free-enterprise system."

"That's Betty," said Maggie Moorehead, the other customer who'd been in the store during the bag-lady debacle. "Surely you've seen her around the neighborhood?"

I found the name tag and pulled it out so I could take a look at it. It said the bag belonged to Jake Benson at O'Brien and Van Dyke, a law firm on our pickup-and-delivery route to businesses in the area. I couldn't put a face to the name, which probably meant Benson never came in the store in person.

Maggie, who's a tall, slim brunette, stretched across the

counter in an effort to look inside the bag. "What in the world is it?" Her hair, which she wore in a straight, turned-under style favored by TV anchorwomen, fell in front of her eyes, and she pulled it back behind her ears so it wouldn't obstruct her view. "The way Betty talked, it must be an Armani suit at the very least."

I wasn't surprised that she would speak in terms of designer labels, since she's the manager of a high-fashion dress salon, located in a fancy shopping area north of the mall.

David was leaning over the counter, too, in an effort to see what all the fuss was about. As for me, I never got to the label. When I dug down inside the bag, the only thing I saw was blood. It popped up at me like a big red flag.

CHAPTER 2

I yanked the drawstring back in place and dropped the bag on the floor. This was not something I wanted to share with my customers.

"Sorry, Maggie, but it's no Armani. Just a worn-out old suit that someone must have thrown away." I hadn't actually touched the blood, but as hard as I tried, I couldn't keep from wiping my hands on my navy-blue wool skirt.

I turned to David and gave him what I hoped was my most dazzling smile. "So, David, don't tell me you've been out jogging on a cold day like this?"

The man seemed bewildered by my quick change of subject, but he finally looked down at his outfit. The jogging suit was tight and didn't do a thing for him, even though it looked expensive. It was the same color as his skin and hair and made him look tan all over.

"Oh, this." He tugged at the knit fabric. "I just came from a workout at the gym, and I thought I'd pick up my cleaning on the way to work."

I put the name David Withers into our computer, and his

account number and current order came up on the screen: a suit, a sports jacket, two pairs of pants, and five shirts on hangers. The computer even showed where the clothes were stored, thanks to a scanning gun we use to zap across the bar codes on each slot of our conveyor.

"I'll have your order in just a minute," I said, anxious to get him out of there so I could take a better look at the suit.

I went through the door into our plant and pushed a control switch to start the conveyor. Too bad Betty wasn't here to see it when it was moving. It went spinning around the ceiling of the call office like a carousel at a carnival.

When I collected David's order, I returned to the counter with the clothes. "That'll be thirty dollars and eighty-five cents."

He pulled out his money, and we settled the bill. Unfortunately he didn't seem to be in any hurry to leave. "Could I have a word with you about something else?" He moved to the end of the counter, away from where Lucille was still waiting on Maggie.

David's my insurance agent, so I figured he was going to tell me that my premiums would be going up next year. I followed him reluctantly.

"Uh . . ." He hesitated, then continued in a low voice. "We're having an office Christmas party this Friday night, and I need a date. I was wondering if you might be interested in going with me."

Maybe it was my anxiety about the suit or relief about the insurance, but for the time being, I couldn't think of a single reason why not. "Sure, that might be fun."

"The party begins at six-thirty, so why don't you tell me where you live . . ." He started to grab for a pen, then realized he didn't have any pockets.

"Maybe we could talk about it later." I waved my hand in a vague motion behind me. "I have an emergency out in the plant."

"No problem, Mandy. I'll talk to you later."

I watched him as he walked out the door, and it was only then that I thought of several reasons I shouldn't have said I'd go out with him. One was that I'd always had an unwritten rule against dating customers. The other was that I didn't know if I wanted to spend an entire evening listening to him talk about his ex-wife, Peg, whom I didn't even know.

I swear sometimes customers treat dry cleaners as if we're psychiatrists, and I'd heard all about David's broken heart once his wife left him and he'd started having to handle his own clothes-care maintenance. I'd even thought of telling him about my own divorce, but he'd said once that I reminded him a little of Peg, and I didn't want to appear to be a vindictive ex-wife.

Maggie grabbed her clothes off the rail and came over to me as she started to leave. "Some people sure don't know what colors look good on them."

I'd bent down for the bag, but I stood up again. "I'm sorry. What did you say?"

"That poor guy looks like someone walking along a nude beach in nothing but his dress shoes." She chuckled as she motioned at David. She'd obviously noticed his all-tan attire, but missed the part about the date we'd just made. I doubt if she'd have said anything otherwise.

Actually his jogging suit made me hope he was pulling himself out of his post-parting-with-Peg doldrums. If he'd started working out, maybe it would motivate me to begin an exercise program too. Perhaps we could even do it together . . . .

"He's been a little distracted ever since his divorce," I said, trying to defend him.

Another man, about David's height, had collared David outside the store and was saying something to him. David seemed to want to get away, and I couldn't blame him.

I usually tried to avoid Eric Jenkins myself. He looks like a cocky bantam rooster on steroids, and he always bores people with his stories about bodybuilding. He also likes to tell dirty jokes and generally disrupt business when he comes into the cleaners. Still, I debated whether to disappear into the back room before he saw me or to stick around to talk to him.

He was, after all, a lawyer at O'Brien and Van Dyke, and I was sure he'd know Jake Benson of the mysterious dirty-clothes bag. But he was also a big mouth who would like nothing better than to spread the news all over the neighborhood about Betty's foray into the cleaners with the bloody suit.

Just in time I came to my senses. I left Lucille to hold down the counter, albeit reluctantly, grabbed the bag by its drawstring, and escaped into the back of the plant. Better to call Jake Benson directly. I just hoped he was alive and well and able to explain what had happened to the suit.

I took another peek inside the bag as soon as I reached my office. The suit was a gray pinstripe, and yep, that was blood all right. If it looked like blood and had the metallic smell of blood, no way was it food coloring.

And even though we get bloodstained garments occasionally, this was different. It was the first time I'd had something come in under such mysterious circumstances. Never mind that Betty had snared the suit out of a trash can only moments before a garbage truck came to haul it off to a landfill. How had the suit gotten from the law firm in one of our dirty-clothes bags in the first place?

I left the bag on the floor and turned on the computer. I keyed in Jake Benson's name, and according to our special dry-cleaning program, I could see I'd been right. He wasn't one of our in-store customers, which explained why the name hadn't rung any bells. Except for one trip to the cleaners for alterations, he'd used our pickup-and-delivery service exclusively.

I jotted down his office number and dialed the phone.

"O'Brien and Van Dyke, Attorneys-at-Law," a sultry voice said. "How may I help you?"

"I'd like to speak to Jake Benson."

"If you'll give me your name and phone number, he'll return your call." I wondered if the woman looked as sexy as she sounded and if there were elocution classes for receptionists so they could sound flirtatious even when they were saying the most innocuous things.

"Look, it's very important that I talk to him right now."

"I'm sorry, but he isn't available at the moment." Her voice was only a husky whisper now.

I hurried before it drifted away altogether. "I wonder if you could tell me if he came to work this morning."

"Well, yes, but he's not taking any calls."

Thank God, that meant he wasn't dead. I have to admit that I'd had visions of him lying in an alley somewhere, stripped of his clothes and bleeding to death at this very moment.

"Please have him call Mandy Dyer at Dyer's Cleaners," I said. "The number is five-five-KLEAN."

"Five-five-KLEAN?" Sexy Voice spelled it out, but I thought I detected just a touch of sarcasm in her sugary tone.

"That's right—five-five-K-L-E-A-N." I'm no fan of the way people use letters for phone numbers, but I'll do anything to promote the business and get it to turn a profit. Maybe then I can get back to my art.

"I'll see that he gets the message."

"Just a minute." I flipped through my Rolodex and found the O'Brien and Van Dyke card. "Could I speak to Karen Morelli while I'm on the line?"

She was the office manager, whom I'd contacted when we started the route. She'd set up a closet in the law firm where we could pick up the employees' dirty clothes and return the clean ones three days later. Maybe she could tell me if someone had ransacked the closet.

"I'm sorry, but *no one* can come to the phone right now." The receptionist's voice was beginning to lose most of its sensual quality by the time she hung up.

No one? Things were getting weird.

I punched in numbers on the computer. Part of the dry-cleaning program tells us what clothes each customer has sent us during the past year. The idea is that we can check back when a customer says we've lost a garment and see if we actually did. Usually they've just misplaced it at home.

No gray pinstripes under Benson's name. He seemed to be more the sports-jacket type. I noted the time he'd been in to have his pants shortened, and just for the heck of it I went to our alteration tickets, which are filed by date. He'd had our seamstress shorten a pair of slacks to thirty five inches at the inseam.

"I wonder. . . ." I took the bag and went back to one of the spotting boards by our two dry-cleaning machines. McKenzie Rivers, my cleaner-spotter, wasn't around.

I pulled on a pair of latex gloves because, when we do get bloodstained garments, we take precautions just like anyone else who works around blood. I removed the suit and laid it on a stainless steel spotting board.

"Damn." There was even more blood than I'd thought. It covered the front of the jacket like a dark red shroud, some of it not even dry yet, and there was a spattering on the pants. Too much blood for a nosebleed, and no rips or tears to indicate an accident.

I checked the label under the inside breast pocket to see if the suit was expensive. Not an Armani as Maggie had speculated. Not even close. It was a private label made for JCPenney, but I guess *expensive* is a relative term when it comes to a bag lady and the manager of a high-fashion dress salon.

I found a tape measure and checked the inseam on the pants. Only thirty inches. No way did the suit belong to Jake Benson, unless he'd shrunk.

So if the suit wasn't Benson's, whom did it belong to? I tried the pockets. Maybe something inside would give me a clue to the owner. People leave a lot of strange things in their pockets, not just business cards and scraps of papers but money, matchbooks, swizzle sticks, condoms, traces of strange powdery substances, and funny-looking pills. Sometimes I even agree with Lucille. I think we could do personality profiles and find missing persons from clothes and the things people leave inside.

But there was nothing in the outside pockets, only a few

fuzz balls and a trace of tobacco. I went for the inside pocket, careful to avoid the blood. It was my last hope.

"What the hell is that?" McKenzie Rivers's voice boomed from just behind me.

I jumped guiltily, the way I had when he'd scolded me as a kid for some malfeasance around the plant. I felt like a pickpocket caught in the act.

"Hey, Mack, I'm glad you're here." I pulled my hand out and looked around at the tall black man who is also my production manager and the person who'd convinced me that I could actually run the cleaners after Uncle Chet died. "Betty found this in a trash can this morning. It was in one of our dirty-clothes bags from a business on our route."

"*What* business?"

The way he asked the question made a chill run up my spine.

"O'Brien and Van Dyke, the law firm," I said.

"Jee-sus!" Mack's also a part-time actor, and the word carried through the plant as if he were playing to the back row of a theater. "I was just in the break room, and the TV's on. There was a news bulletin about Harrison Van Dyke, the high-powered lawyer. He was stabbed to death in his office last night, and one of the cops said the place looked like a slaughterhouse."

CHAPTER 3

"It can't be Harrison Van Dyke," I blurted. "He was out of town all weekend."

Mack looked at me as if I had a couple of buttons missing. "And just how would you know something like that?"

"Agnes Burley, the Van Dykes' maid, was in here Friday with a bunch of his suits and said she needed them by the time her boss got home from one of his business trips today. That's how."

Mack shook his head at the unreliability of my third-hand information and removed a load of clothes from one of the cleaning machines, which looks like a front-load washer only larger.

That gave me a chance to get in touch with my own reality. Van Dyke and his wife, Sybil, were among my best customers, but it wasn't as if I knew them personally. In fact I'd only seen the tall, distinguished-looking Van Dyke once when he'd come into the cleaners to inquire about cleaning some Navajo rugs. I was quite certain he'd had more than a thirty-inch inseam, though. As for his red-haired wife, I knew her only from newspaper pictures of her at charity events and from her incredibly petite clothes.

"I'll call the police," I said, pulling off the gloves and throwing them away.

Mack nodded his head. "That would probably be a wise idea."

Dry cleaners, unlike pawnshop owners, aren't required by law to notify the police when something comes to them under suspicious circumstances, but I knew my civic duty.

I went to my office, looked up the regular number for the police department instead of using 911, and explained the situation to a man on the other end of the line. He said he'd notify someone to come and pick up the suit, but while I waited, I found myself drawn back to the suit like a moth to a porch light.

"There aren't any cuts or holes to indicate entrance wounds," I said, confirming my first thought that it wasn't Van Dyke's suit.

"So maybe it's the killer's suit," Mack said from the other spotting board, where he was removing some wine stains from an emerald-green cocktail dress. "But I wouldn't handle it anymore if I were you."

"I know." I leaned down closer to the jacket, not touching it. "Oh, wait. Here's a hole just below the left breast pocket with some singed threads around the edges."

"You mean like a bullet hole?" He couldn't resist coming over to take a look.

"No, sorry. I guess it's a cigarette burn. The hole doesn't go through the lining."

We continued to stare down at the suit together.

"It's a few years old, don't you think?" I asked. "The material looks worn."

Mack nodded.

It was too bad men's fashions don't change the way women's do or we could have pinned down the age more precisely.

"And look here." I pointed at the button at the waistline of the jacket. "The fabric is pulled around the button . . ."

Now Mack was into playing dry-cleaning detective too. "There's a short blond hair on the lapel."

I bent down until I was only a few inches from where he was pointing. "I think it's light brown, and whoever the guy is, he needs to get some Head and Shoulders shampoo. There's dandruff on the collar."

Mack laughed. "Guess that narrows it down."

"There was nothing in the pockets."

"The cops probably aren't going to like the fact that you went through the pockets."

Mack had always seemed a little wary of the police, and when I was a kid, I had fantasized that he had some dark mysterious past in the Northwest. That was after I found out in geography class that there was a real McKenzie River in Oregon.

But maybe it was a stage name, since his real love was acting. Unfortunately, like me and my painting, he couldn't make a living at it, so he expended his excess creative energy at the spotting board, where he was a genius at removing stains with a steam gun and a variety of solutions in squirt bottles. The more fragile the fabric and the more difficult the stain, the better he liked it.

He returned to the silk dress, and I continued to contemplate the suit.

"What I'd really like to do is remove the blood," I said. Mack didn't even look over at me. He knew I wouldn't do it.

Strangely enough, blood is one of the easiest stains to remove. All it takes is water or an ice cube, but because water can damage some of the fabrics we have to deal with, we use a solution called Scram Blood. That and a spatula made from bone, plus a little elbow grease.

"Out, damned spot." I waved my hands over the suit as if to zap away the blood, and this time Mack did glance my way.

That's what he used to say when I was a kid as he removed the stains, his deep baritone voice carrying clear to the front counter. I'd loved it. I didn't find out until junior high—about the same time I learned about the McKenzie River in Oregon—that it was a line from *Macbeth*. Up until then I'd liked him because he cussed.

"I keep telling you it has to come from the diaphragm. OUT, DAMNED SPOT." His voice echoed through the plant.

"Mandy." The voice of Ann Marie, who'd arrived at work to relieve Lucille at the counter, came from the opposite direction, not as loud as Mack's but high-pitched and squeaky. "There's a man out front who says he's a policeman and wants to see you."

I tucked my gray silk blouse into the waistband of my skirt, smoothed down my hair, and went to greet him. It never hurts to look your best when you go to meet the law.

"He's a real hunk," she added when I reached her. Ann Marie's an overenthusiastic teenager who works for me in the mornings and goes to school afternoons. She'd be filling in full-time during Christmas vacation.

When I reached the call office, the man was looking at the

mural I'd done for my uncle on one of the walls when the plant opened five years ago.

The mural is a history of fashion from the turn of the century to the present, and I'd used elongated figures in the style of El Greco. I'd read once that the famous Spanish painter may have had an astigmatism, and that's why his people were always so tall and thin. Other art scholars said it was because he was trying to make his religious subjects seem otherworldly. Me, I was just trying to make the figures look good in their clothes.

"I'm Detective Stan Foster," the man said after I introduced myself.

He appeared to be in his late thirties, and he could have been a model for my mural, he was so tall and thin. He was at least six foot four, but the thing that was different from my soft, rounded people was that he was all straight lines. A square jaw, a Roman nose, eyes like slits as they squinted at me, and a cleft in his chin that was a shadowy slash. The only thing that wasn't straight was his blond, curly hair. In fact he looked a little like a young Clint Eastwood, but with a perm and the clothes sense of Columbo. In other words he was a rumpled hunk.

"I understand you called us about a suit that may have something to do with the homicide at O'Brien and Van Dyke law firm." Foster flipped through a small notebook. "According to my report, someone found it and brought it to you because it was in one of your laundry bags."

I nodded. "If you'll come with me, I'll give it to you."

I led him through the plant. Lucille had finished marking in clothes for the moment and was pulling clear polyethylene garment bags down over completed orders. I had to push some of the clothes aside to get by the rails of cleaning that waited to be assembled and bagged. Once through them, four employees were pressing other garments and two women were at the shirt press. Steam was rising like sulfur from the geysers at Yellowstone until we walked by. Work came to a halt as everyone wondered who the new guy was. Foster eyed the suit suspiciously when we got to the spotting board. "Why did you remove it from the bag?"

"I didn't know it had so much blood on it until I took it out, and I didn't hear about the murder until later." I pointed to the floor where I'd tossed the yellow nylon bag with our logo on it. "The name tag says the bag belongs to Jake Benson, one of our customers at O'Brien and Van Dyke."

"Anyone else handle the suit?" Foster looked over at Mack, who was busy at the spotting board.

"No, just me." I didn't introduce the two men. If Mack was wanted somewhere, the way I'd feared as a child, I didn't want to draw attention to him.

"I'll have to get our crime-lab unit over here to collect the evidence," Foster said. "Where's your phone?"

I started to lead the way.

"Just tell me where it is and see that no one touches the suit while I'm gone."

I told him to go around the corner of the dry-cleaning machines to my office. McKenzie just kept spraying and brushing.

Foster was gone for a few minutes. When he returned, he had his notebook ready and his pen poised above it. "First, I need to know how you came into possession of the suit."

I described how Betty had brought the bag to me that morning, but I could tell he was disappointed that I didn't know where she'd found it.

"Did she mention finding anything else in the trash can?"

I shook my head.

"Well, do you know her last name?"

"All I know is Betty." I thought of giving Bag Lady as a last name, but I figured he might not appreciate it.

"Any idea where she stays at night?"

"No, but she always comes around to the back of the cleaners every morning. We give her doughnuts and coffee."

"Really." He looked surprised. I didn't know if it was because I gave her handouts or because I gave them to a bag lady and hadn't offered anything to him.

"Would you like some coffee, by the way?"

He declined. "Can you give me a description of her?"

We were interrupted by the arrival of the crime-lab crew at the back door. Foster explained to the two men what he needed and then turned to me.

"They have to photograph the suit and bag in the condition they were received, and then they'll bag up the evidence and take it with them," he said. "Meanwhile, why don't we finish the interview in your office?"

I nodded reluctantly. I'd wanted to watch what the crime-lab people did, but I followed him to the office and moved some clothes out of a gold chair that matched the two in the call office. The clothes were problem garments, and I needed to call the owners.

"Why don't you sit there?" I said. He'd been eyeing the swivel chair behind my desk, but I figured that would put me at a disadvantage.

Foster sat down, but the gold chair was too small for him. He looked like Gulliver in the land of the Lilliputians. I went around the desk and sat in the swivel chair.

He looked at his notebook. "You were about to give me a description of the woman."

I wondered if he was ready for this. "She's about my height, five-five, brown eyes, gray hair, a couple of missing teeth, and she wears a gray knit cap and"— I paused—"and a brown Hefty bag."

"A—what?" He sat up straighter in the chair.

"You know, a Hefty bag. The same way some people wear ponchos or plastic rain gear over their clothes."

He stopped writing in his notebook as if trying to regain his cop composure. "When she brought you the suit, did she say anything about seeing the person who threw it in the trash can?"

"No. Well, I'm not sure. She said—" I tried to recall her exact words. "She said, 'Why would the guy throw away a good suit like that—unless it was stolen?' "

"And you didn't ask her anything else—either about the guy or about the blood on the suit?"

"I didn't know anything about the blood at the time," I reminded him. "I just gave her twenty dollars for returning the bag, and she left."

"You gave her money?" He put his hand to his head as if he couldn't believe what he was hearing. "Well, I doubt if we'll be able to find her now. She's probably off on a week-long drunk."

It sounded like something Uncle Chet would have said, but all the same, Foster took time out to call and ask that some patrol cars cruise the neighborhood looking for her.

I refused to feel guilty about corrupting a bag lady.

"Tell me about these bags of yours," he said. "Why did this one say Jake Benson and give the law firm, not his home address?"

I hurried through the procedure of how we give them to customers on our pickup route to businesses in the area. "We supply empty bags with blank name tags on them, and when a new customer wants to send us something, he fills out the tag with his name and the office where he works, puts his dirty clothes in the bag, and our driver picks it up. We clean the clothes, launder the bag, and return it with the order so that he can use the same bag the next time he wants to send us something." I could tell I was boring him, but I'd saved the best for last. "The important thing is that we have a closet we use at O'Brien and Van Dyke so that we can pick up and deliver the clothes without disrupting business. Have you taken a look at it yet?"

"A closet?" It was like a lightbulb going off above his head. "Where is it?"

I told him the location, and he made another call and asked someone named Officer Reilly to secure the closet until he could check it out.

While I was on a roll, I said, "And even if you don't find Betty right away, we still know a lot about the person who wore the suit."

Foster looked puzzled. "About this Jake Benson, you mean?"

I leaned toward him in a gesture of sharing my expertise. "I don't think the suit belongs to Mr. Benson."

"Oh, you know him personally?"

"No, but we did some alterations for him, and he's taller, just like Mr. Van Dyke was. From the size of the suit, I'd say the owner was about five-eight or five-nine."

"You checked out the suit?"

"Yes." I felt I needed to let him know what I'd done—so why not put it in the best possible light by telling him what

I'd discovered? "I went through the pockets to try to find out who the owner was, but there wasn't anything there."

He ran his hands through his hair. "You shouldn't have done that."

"Once I heard about the murder, I never touched it again."

"You should have left it for our crime lab, Ms. Dyer."

"I used gloves—"

He put up a hand to stop me. "That's not the point. There's a chain of custody that the police need to establish to make sure the evidence is admissible in court."

"Don't you at least want to know what I found out?" I asked. "For instance the suit wasn't new, and at some point the owner had gained weight."

"We'll let the lab make that determination, Ms. Dyer."

Once I got going, I couldn't seem to stop myself. "There was a blond or light brown hair on the collar—"

I could tell he was losing patience with me. "Look, Ms. Dyer, we're not playing Sherlock Holmes and Dr. Watson here."

So much for sharing my expertise. I kept the information about the cigarette burn and the dandruff to myself. My only satisfaction was that for the moment I knew more about the owner of the suit than he did.

He unfolded himself from the chair like a basketball player finally called into the game. "Well, thanks for your help."

I started to escort him back through the plant when I had an idea. "Look, maybe I could help you by taking a look at the closet." After all, I told myself, I do have a responsibility to my customers whose clothes are in the closet.

He looked dubious.

"Theoretically the closet is our property, and we have a liability for what's inside."

I wasn't actually sure if that was true, but he looked less dubious.

"I might be able to tell you if something's missing."

"Okay, okay," he said, if a bit begrudgingly.

I went back into the office, and on the theory that it never hurts to advertise, I grabbed my white blazer with the words *Dyer's Cleaners* embroidered on a pocket. It didn't occur to me until later that it also might advertise my involvement in the case—however remote—to the killer.

CHAPTER 4

I led the way out of the cleaners, pushing aside cleaned and freshly pressed clothes as I did.

Once Foster made up his mind I could go with him, he seemed to make an effort to be pleasant.

"This is kind of interesting," he said. "I've never been in the back of a dry cleaners before." He still had his pen out, the point protracted as he waved it around the plant.

I had visions of him getting ink all over the clothes as we squeezed by them. "Would you mind putting that thing away? It's a dangerous weapon back here."

"Oh, sorry." He looked embarrassed as he jammed the pen into his shirt pocket.

I could tell this guy was an "outie." He didn't retract the ballpoint when he put the pen back in his pocket. There was a glob of black ink at the bottom of the pocket.

"You really should bring your shirts to us," I said. "We can get those ink stains out from around your pockets."

He looked down sheepishly. "I'm always doing that." He removed the pen and pushed in the point.

After I told one of the counter people that I'd be gone for an hour or so, we went outside to his unmarked car. There was a threat of snow in the air, and I shivered as I climbed inside.

"We'll have the heat going in just a minute," he said.

"I guess I should have brought a coat." I didn't tell him that the reason I hadn't was that I'd worn my old down-filled jacket to work today. It's green and purple and is my starving-artist protest against always having to dress up and look nice.

Unfortunately dressing well is one of the occupational hazards of the job. People aren't going to be confident in your ability to keep their clothes in tip-top shape if you go around looking like a candidate for Mr. Blackwell's worst-dressed list. The old jacket just didn't seem the thing to wear to a law firm.

Foster swung over a block to First Avenue and headed toward the high-rise building that housed O'Brien and Van Dyke law offices on the top floor. The new Cherry Creek Mall was to our left and was the pride and joy of Denver's elite. Denver finally had a Lord & Taylor and a Saks Fifth Avenue as two of the anchor stores.

Foster cleared his throat. "I was just wondering. How do you get the ink out—around the pockets, I mean?"

I don't usually share trade secrets, but maybe this way he'd feel he owed me one. "Well, if you don't want to bring your shirts to us, you might try hair spray on the ink, then wash the shirt in hot, soapy water. It generally does the trick."

"Thanks, I'll try that."

He drove past the original Cherry Creek Shopping Center, which had looked like a 1990s version of a ghost town when it was first abandoned for the new location. Now some restaurants were going into the front of the place, and it didn't seem so forlorn.

But the office building beyond the center looked empty. It had those tinted windows that you can't see through, as if it surely must be hiding something ugly inside.

This time it was. I could see all the police cars in the parking lot as we drew closer. The last of the TV trucks that had probably been there earlier was just pulling out of the parking lot.

"I don't know if this might be of help," I said, "but the woman who marks in the clothes used to find long blond hairs on some of Mr. Van Dyke's clothes."

Foster glanced over at me as if he couldn't believe I was analyzing clothes again.

"Van Dyke had silver-white hair, as I recall, and his wife is a redhead. I just thought the blond hairs might be significant."

"I didn't know the dry-cleaning business could be so interesting." Foster shook his head as he swung into the lot.

When he shut off the ignition, he opened his notebook and wrote in it. I wondered if he was making a note about the blond hairs or simply jotting down Mandy's Helpful Hint for Ink Removal. Probably I should stick to clothes-care counseling.

We got out of the car, and by the time we reached the entrance to the building, I was shaking again. This time I think it was a combination of the cold and the fact that I was about to see the crime scene where a person I knew, if mostly from his wearing apparel, had been killed.

The elevator whisked us up to the twelfth floor, where a uniformed policeman was checking IDs at the door.

"She's with me," Foster said as we went past him into the reception area of the law firm. "Would you wait for a minute while I check on something?" He pointed to a spot on the gray carpet as if it were X'd in tape for an actor to stand on during a take of a TV cop show.

He went over and conferred with a uniformed cop at the door to a conference room to my left. I could see a lot of people sitting around the table inside, not saying anything. One of them was Eric Jenkins, the cocky bantam rooster of a lawyer I'd avoided earlier this morning. Jenkins gave me a puzzled look and a furtive wave of recognition.

I stood on the invisible X on the rug and looked around the reception area. The law firm occupied the whole top floor, so we'd stepped right off the elevator into the waiting room.

What I remembered most from the other time I'd been here to set up the delivery service were the Navajo rugs. They adorned the walls like tapestries. The color scheme of gray, black, and red had been built around them and seemed to give the room a somber look now that I knew the man who collected the rugs was dead.

At the reception desk an attractive blonde worked the phone. She had to be Ms. Sexy Voice. She was wearing a low-cut blouse under a peach-colored suit that looked as if it belonged on someone in a higher tax bracket, and I have to admit, I hadn't seen that much cleavage since Loni Anderson took the calls at WKRP in Cincinnati.

The woman ignored me as she punched buttons with the tip of her pencil and wrote down messages on a pad.

That was fine with me. It gave me time to mentally measure her long blond hair. Yep, it was about the same length as the hairs on Van Dyke's clothes, and I could picture her with her head on his shoulder as they set off for a weekend tryst somewhere.

I remembered what Agnes Burley, the Van Dyke maid, had said on one of her visits to the cleaners. "I can't figure why he'd be away on *business* every weekend," she'd whispered to me across the counter, "unless it's monkey business he's up to."

The remark had struck a responsive chord in me, and I'd had to agree with her conclusion. After all, I'd been married to Larry, a law student who'd told me how he needed to get away by himself on weekends to study for the bar. Unfortunately he passed a bar too many on the way and fell in love with a lady lawyer he met in one. Together they'd set up a practice in Aspen.

Foster stopped at Ms. Sexy Voice's desk on his way back to me. "Are you still keeping a record of all the calls, Ms. Leyton?"

"Yes, but please, just call me Pamela," she purred. She really should give lessons to my cat, the most unfriendly feline in the world.

While Foster checked the calls, a tall, dark-haired man came out of a door to my right and got on the elevator. A balding, stoop-shouldered man was summoned from the conference room, crossed the reception area, and entered the same door. Both men gave me a curious look as they went by, and I couldn't help wondering if the first one had been Jake Benson. He was tall enough to have a thirty five-inch inseam. The other guy didn't fit my profile for the owner of the suit, either, but I was sure he'd been in the cleaners at some point.

"Thanks, Ms. Leyton." Foster put down the list of phone calls while I took satisfaction in the fact that he'd resisted calling her by her first name. I wondered if he'd caught the significance of her long blond hair.

He motioned for me to follow him down a hallway to her right. Pamela's perfume wafted up to me as we passed her. I think it was Obsession.

"Her hair's about the right color and length," I whispered to him as we reached the closet.

"Thanks, Ms. Dyer, for your observation." I thought he tried to hide a smile as he slipped on another pair of latex gloves and opened the door, then moved aside so I could take a look.

The place was a mess. There was a jumble of clothes on the floor along with a bunch of our empty dirty-clothes bags. A couple of cleaned orders were on a rod above them, but the poly garment bags that covered them had been ripped open to expose women's clothing inside.

"So what do you think?" Foster asked.

"I assume those are dirty clothes on the floor." I bent down to take a closer look.

"Don't touch anything," he warned.

I drew back my hand guiltily. "Ordinarily they'd be in the bags with the names of the owners written on the tags of the individual bags."

He waited for me to continue.

"Maybe . . ." I hesitated, looking up at him. "Could you tell me one thing? Was Mr. Van Dyke—uh—wearing clothes?"

At least Foster took the question seriously. "Yes, he was fully dressed."

Okay, I'd already been sure the bloody suit wasn't his because of the size, not to mention the fact that Van Dyke had most of his suits custom-tailored, but I had to ask. And frankly, from what Van Dyke's maid had said, I wouldn't have been surprised if Van Dyke had been found lying on the floor, stark naked, after one of his weekend liaisons.

"So the bloody suit has to be the killer's." I rose to my feet, but as I did, my knees creaked. I really needed to get more exercise. "And when he got blood all over it, he didn't know what to do. He didn't want to be seen leaving the building that way, so he was—well, maybe he knew about the closet—and he went through it looking for something that would fit him." Yeah, that made sense to me. "Then he changed his clothes, put the bloody suit in one of the bags, and threw it away after he left the building."

Foster didn't compliment me on my deductive skills, but I was pleased with my own scenario.

"Okay," he said, "so by that theory, one of your customers here at the law firm should be missing an item of clothing from this closet. Is there something in the bags that will tell us what each person was sending you?" He had his pen out, ready to take notes again.

I hated to disappoint him. "No, we don't have our customers make a list of what they send us. We do that when the bags come into the plant. The whole idea is speed and convenience to the customer."

"I thought you said you could tell me if something was missing." He was getting irritated.

"Well, I didn't know everything would be dumped out. I thought maybe a couple of bags . . ."

"So we'll have to ask the customers to identify all these clothes"— he shook his head as he motioned to the closet floor —"and see what's missing?"

I nodded. "If you want to find out what the killer wore when he left the building."

I wasn't sure if it was that important, but if the police would sort out the clothes for us, it would save us a lot of trouble later at the plant.

"I probably should mention that dry-cleaning customers are infamous for not remembering what they send us." I'd debated even bringing up the subject, but I decided he should be forewarned.

"You're kidding," he said as if he couldn't believe what he was hearing.

I shrugged. "Just be prepared for that possibility."

A uniformed policeman approached us. He took Foster aside and whispered something to him.

At the conclusion of their conversation Foster told him to get the lab crew to go over the closet and inventory the clothes. Then he turned to me. "There's no sign of the bag lady around the neighborhood. Anything else you can think of that might help us find her?"

"You mean the Hefty bag isn't enough?"

"Right. The woman in the Hefty bag. I'm sure no one even notices her face when she's wearing a get-up like that. All she needs to do is take off the bag and she's incognito." He indicated with his hand that I should precede him back through the hall to the reception area. "Incidentally, don't say anything about this to anyone, and the minute the woman shows up at the cleaners, you call us."

I agreed and started to leave.

"We wouldn't want a possible witness to turn up dead in an alley somewhere . . ."

I stopped, and he almost ran into me. "You really think she's in danger?"

"If the killer thinks she saw him—or she could always

drink herself into a stupor on that twenty dollars you gave her, pass out, and freeze to death."

Talk about making a person feel guilty for something that hadn't even happened yet, and pray to God, never would. "I'll call you," I promised.

I continued on down the hallway, then stopped again. This time Foster did run into me just as we reached Sexy Voice's desk.

"Maybe I could draw you a picture of Betty."

He looked at me in astonishment as he pulled me away from Pamela's interested, upturned face. "Oh, sure, draw me a picture of someone in a Hefty bag."

I probably shouldn't have volunteered, but once I had, my honor was at stake. "I can do it. I used to draw sketches of people at street fairs." It had been in my bohemian period before I had to start dressing up and looking nice. "I was good at it."

He thought it over. "Was that mural at the cleaners yours?"

"Yes."

"I hate to say it, but they didn't look like real people to me."

And here I'd thought he'd been admiring the mural, but I guess he hadn't. "They weren't supposed to look like real people. If I'd wanted them to look like real people, they'd have looked like real people."

He seemed taken aback by my agitated defense of my art. "Okay, draw me a picture of the bag lady." He got out a business card and handed it to me. "And don't forget to call me—day or night—if Betty shows up." He handed me the card and jammed his pen back in his pocket, once again forgetting to retract the point.

CHAPTER
5

I t was seven o'clock when I finally locked up the plant. The snow that had been threatening all day still hadn't started, but there was enough moisture in the air that the windshield and back window of the Dyer's Cleaners van had a thin sheet of ice on them. I had to get out a scraper to clear them off.

My production crew had gone home hours before, and my two afternoon counter people, Sarah and Theresa, both had rides waiting for them in the parking lot. Theresa's husband offered to stay until I was safely locked in the van, but I waved him off.

It probably wouldn't have hurt to have him as lookout, considering the fact that Foster seemed to think the killer might come around the cleaners looking for Betty. That had been Foster's final comment before he had a patrolman drive me back to work earlier in the day. However, no one was looking for me. Why kill the messenger. Right?

All the same, I felt better when I was safely locked inside the van, which is normally used for our pickup-and-delivery work. When it was not in service, I used it as my personal transportation because, just like my snappy blazer with the embroidered name on the lapel, I felt that way I advertised the business every place I went. One of my customers even asked me once if we had a fleet of trucks because he saw them all over town.

I'd recently revamped the logo, and it was painted on the sides of the van: a golden flower entwined around the *y* in *Dyer's Cleaners* with a "Fresh as a Daisy" slogan underneath. Uncle Chet used to have a hanger dangling from the *y*, but when someone used spray paint to put a slash through it, I decided I didn't want anything to do with hangers. I'm actually a pro-choicer myself, but it just wasn't good business practice to make political statements on the side of the van.

I couldn't help myself. I kept looking down alleys as I drove north, and took a left at Eighth Avenue, a one-way street heading west toward the mountains. No sign of Betty. Maybe the police had found her by now. A swirl of wind tossed an empty garbage can into my path, almost like a sign that she was out there someplace.

At Downing I turned north and headed to Capitol Hill near downtown Denver, where there were some homeless shelters. What I really hoped was that Betty was safely tucked away in one, not out wandering the streets or drinking cheap wine in an alley.

I had to park a block away from my apartment, which is one of the disadvantages of living where I do, especially since it's one of the highest crime areas in the city. To protect myself against the cold if not the muggers, I zipped up my old down-filled jacket, which Mack once said made me look like the top half of a sleeping bag. So much for dressing up and looking nice. I made a run for my building.

My apartment's on the top floor of an old Victorian house. It's an attic really, just one big room, but it has a sky-light and windows on all sides and makes a great studio.

I unlocked the door when I reached the third floor.

"Meow." Uncle Chet's cat sat back on his haunches and gave me the evil eye.

"Hi, Spot," I said.

It was another trade joke. Spot had long golden hair and nary a spot on him. My uncle had found him in the parking lot outside his downtown store years ago and named the kitten Spot because he thought it was funny for a cleaners that prides itself on removing spots.

I'd inherited the cat, along with the cleaners, but the big male tabby didn't seem to like me. Actually, Spot wasn't that fond of anyone, including my uncle.

When Uncle Chet found Spot, the tiny kitten had just been born. His eyes were closed, and he had been abandoned by his mother. My uncle nursed him from a toy baby bottle, but the cat's chances of survival still had to have been about a thousand to one.

Uncle Chet was sure the cat had some deformities, perhaps even arthritis, and that's why he didn't like to be petted. But Spot was so pretty that people always wanted to stroke his golden coat. There were disastrous consequences to those who tried.

It hadn't helped Spot's disposition several years later when Uncle Chet moved the cat out to the new store. Spot took to spending most of his time on that gold velvet chair in the dry-cleaning office. He blended right in with the chair, and if anyone came near, he would hiss and take a swipe at them. I finally decided maybe he'd be happier in my apartment. I was wrong.

Spot cut a wide swath around me, no rubbing around ankles for this one, as he went to his food bowl. I got out some expensive cat food I'd bought at the vet's, thinking maybe if I improved his diet, it would help his disposition. It hadn't worked. I personally thought he just liked being cantankerous, but I was careful not to pet him in case Uncle Chet had been right about the arthritis.

He gave me a dirty look when I poured out some dry kitty nibbles, as if to say he'd rather have junk food. He sat back on his haunches again and refused to eat them.

"Maybe you still miss Uncle Chet," I said as I broke down and opened up a foul-smelling can of cat tuna. "I know I do, and I sure wish he'd been around today."

Spot wasn't interested in my problems, but he perked up a little when I scooped some of the tuna into his bowl.

If Uncle Chet hadn't liked strays, he probably never would have taken me on as a project, much less Spot, not to mention the bag lady. My dad, who was Chet's brother and partner, died when I was only a year old, and my mom set out on a lifelong pursuit to find another perfect mate. She'd been married and divorced three times by the time I was a junior in high school, and when she married again and moved to Omaha, I stayed behind with Uncle Chet and his wife so I could finish school. Even before Mom left, I hung around the cleaners a lot. It was better than hanging around all those constantly changing stepfathers.

I never could figure out why Mom seemed to find her identity only through a man. The one time she'd been happy for me was when I married Larry. This from a woman who hadn't "found herself" with any of her first five husbands, although she seemed to be happy now with Number 6, a retired used-car dealer. She called occasionally from their home in Arizona to see if I'd found a fella yet.

She was still disappointed with me that I'd let Larry the Law Student, as he came to be known, get away. I'd worked at a variety of boring office jobs to help him through law school. The plan had been that I'd get to pursue my art once he earned his degree, but of course it didn't work out that way. The only things I had to show for those years of toil were the dark, angry canvases that I'd painted right after he left, plus the fifteen pounds I gained while I sequestered myself away in my apartment with my paintbrushes and oils—and a lot of junk food to ease the pain.

So was it any wonder, I ask you, that I didn't trust lawyers or that I thought the worst of poor Harrison Van Dyke?

"You know, Spot," I said as he cocked his head at me, which was a signal he wanted more of the soft, smelly food. "You're probably the perfect companion for me. We don't get in each other's way and we don't hurt each other."

I fed him another dollop of tuna, got into my grungies—a paint-splattered sweatshirt and jeans—and heated up a "healthy" TV dinner, which I had about as much enthusiasm for as Spot did for his scientifically blended cat food. Unfortunately I didn't have anything better.

I ate the dinner while I thought about the sketch I'd promised Foster. I tried to visualize Betty's face. Think of the overall look. Don't go for your old art teacher's suggestion. "Draw a large egg," she'd said. "Then draw a line across the page halfway down the egg. That's where the eyes will be."

She was right, but that's not the way I liked to do it. I got out a pencil and sketch pad and started with the eyes.

Betty's piercing brown eyes under dark eyebrows. It was funny how some people's eyebrows never turned gray, even when the hair on top of their head did. It reminded me of Harrison Van Dyke's dark eyebrows and prematurely silver-white hair the time I'd talked to him at the cleaners.

I'd never seen Betty without her knit cap, so I drew it in and added gray hair sticking out underneath like patches of crabgrass. I held the sketch out in front of me and squinted at it. Yeah, that looked right.

Spot sat and watched me. He meowed, which was the friendliest sound he ever made. God forbid he would ever purr. He wagged his tail, which would have been a good sign only if he were a dog, the way any self-respecting Spot should be.

I walked over to the window with the fire escape to see if he wanted to go outside. "Out, damned Spot," I said, chuckling at the Mack-Macbeth humor that only a thirteen-year-old could appreciate. But if it worked for stains, why not for cats?

A frigid blast of air rushed inside as Spot jumped onto the ledge, undecided about what he wanted to do.

"It's either in or out," I said. "I'm not keeping the window open for you."

He gave me a contemptuous look and started out. Just then there was a clattering of metal down below. Spot hissed and the fur on his back stood up.

I snatched him inside, and he turned on me, growling as if he really thought he were a dog. He slashed me with a claw on the back of the hand. I dropped him, and he streaked off. "So much for my theory about us not hurting each other," I said.

By the time I got around to taking a look out the window myself, all I saw was a shadow in the alley, but then it merged into the deeper shadows of a garage across the way. I wondered if someone had been on the fire escape a minute before, and the noise we heard was caused when he jumped from the fire escape back to the ground? I felt as if the hairs on my head were standing up like the ones on Spot's back.

Get a grip on yourself, Mandy. It was probably just a neighbor putting out the trash. No need to get in a panic. Not everyone puts bloody suits in trash cans. Or maybe it was some guy scavenging in the cans. That only served to remind me of Betty and what Foster had said about her freezing to death in an alley someplace.

I started to close the window just as the phone rang. I jumped and the window slammed down on my finger. Damn, you're a klutz, Mandy. I yanked my finger out from under the wooden frame, shut the window more carefully, locked it, and pulled down the shade.

By then my answering machine had kicked on. I let it do the talking for me while I surveyed the damage to my finger and the back of my hand where Spot's scratch had started to bleed.

The machine beeped, and I could hear someone breathing at the other end of the line. Wasn't he ever going to say anything? I'd be damned if I'd pick up for a heavy breather. The breathing continued for what seemed like a full minute.

Unable to stand it anymore, I grabbed the phone. I started to ask what the caller wanted. He hung up.

I busied myself by cleaning out the razorlike scratch and covering it with a Band-Aid. I tried not to think of the heavy breather on the answering machine.

When I finally returned to my sketch pad, I started to work on the nose. It wasn't right, so I went to the mouth. I was tempted to give Betty the missing-tooth smile, but I knew that wouldn't work for identification purposes. People just don't go around smiling while they try to elude the police, which I was sure she'd do if she saw them coming after her. I tried for a closed-lips look, but I'd lost the feel for Betty someplace. I was too damned tense. That was the problem.

The phone rang again. My pencil made an involuntary mark across her chin. I jumped up and paced, waiting for the machine to kick on. Who ever heard of a heavy breather on an answering machine? Damned if I'd answer it until I heard who it was. If it was a problem at the plant, then I'd pick up. I had my home number in the window of the cleaners so I could be called in case of an emergency. There was always the danger of a fire in a dry cleaners.

"Hi, this is Mandy Dyer," my recorded voice said. "I'm not able to take your call right now, but if it's a pressing matter or you want to come clean about something, just leave your name and number and I'll get back to you."

The caller hung up again. No heavy breathing this time. Maybe the guy was turned off by the old Dyer sense of humor. It sure didn't sound funny to me tonight.

Perhaps I should record a more dignified message so I don't irritate my callers. By the fourth time the phone rang, I was going crazy.

" . . . and I'll get back to you," I said. Even my recorded voice sounded nervous to me now.

This time a man's voice started talking to the machine. "Yo, Mandy. If you're there, pick up." A pause, but I knew who it was.

Nat Wilcox never bothered to give his name because he was my best friend, but there was no way I was talking to him tonight.

"I'm waiting," he said. Another pause. "I can't imagine that you're out on a night like this."

So much for his confidence in my ability to lead an active social life during the Christmas season.

He sighed. "I guess you really are out someplace. I was sure you were just hiding out and would finally pick up if I kept calling back, but I suppose I'll have to leave a message after all, and you know how I hate these stupid machines."

I felt a sense of relief. So it had been Nat all along.

"I'm on deadline, so if you get home before ten o'clock, call me at the paper. It's important."

Not on your life, ace. Nat's a police reporter on the *Denver Tribune*, and when he's on the scent of a story, he's as pesky as the insect of the same name. I could just picture him running into the newsroom all out of breath and calling me because he'd gotten wind about the bloodstained suit. I was right.

"Look," he said to the machine, "I might as well tell you what I want. I heard you turned over some evidence to the police, and I need to know what it is and where you got it. The police won't say, and I need your help."

Not tonight. Nat and I had been buddies since junior high. With my artistic ability and his writing skills, we'd created our own comic strips. They were about how kids ruled the world, performing feats of derring-do as we solved crimes committed by our elders.

But somewhere along the way Nat got into "reality writing" and investigative reporting. I wasn't about to pick up right now and risk having him drag it out of me about Betty. Not until the police found her and I could quit feeling responsible for her.

"Damn," he said in what appeared to be a frustrated

aside. "Where are you, Mandy?" More silence. "Just call me as soon as you get home. Okay? If it's after ten, call me at home."

Wasn't the guy ever going to get off the machine?

"Now don't forget. You will call me, won't you?"

"In a gnat's eye, Nat," I said to the machine.

There had to be something to that genetic stuff. I sounded just like Uncle Chet with his Dyer's Cleaners and Dyers. Before I became too amused with myself, I began to wonder if it wasn't actually "in a pig's eye" or "when donkeys fly." Oh, well, who cared?

Just hang up, Nat, please, before I'm tempted to pick up the phone and share my stress-induced humor with you. I promise to call you later. Okay?

"Ciao," Nat said finally. Fortunately he writes better than he talks, what with all his clichéd greetings.

I relaxed when the machine finally shut off, and once the tension disappeared, the sketch practically drew itself.

It was the nose that was wrong. I'd kept trying to make it longer than it really was. I gave it a turned-up, pug look, and I knew that was it, but who would ever think of a bag lady with a perky nose?

I traced in smile wrinkles around her eyes and mouth and sat back in satisfaction. It was Betty the Bag Lady, come to life.

As I slipped the sketch into a folder, the phone rang again. I put the folder inside my bag so I wouldn't forget it the next morning and listened to myself for what seemed like the hundredth time. The message got less funny with each repetition. *Beep.* The machine kicked over to its incoming mode.

"Yo, Man." Nat knew I didn't like it when he shortened

my nickname, but of course, that's why he did it when he was aggravated with me.

"Will you just go away, Nat," I said to the answering machine.

"I'm off deadline now, and I was going to stop by to see you on my way home from work. I thought for sure you'd be home by now." There was silence on the line as if he were contemplating what to do next. "Well, maybe I'll just buzz over anyway and wait for you."

"No way, Jose." I could use trite expressions too. "I don't want to see you tonight."

I heard him hang up, and I knew I had about fifteen minutes to get out of here. Either that or go to bed and not answer my door when he arrived. But I was too wired for sleep, so why not go to the plant and do something that had been in the back of my mind all afternoon? I wanted to check the computer to see if any of my other O'Brien and Van Dyke customers had sent us a gray pinstriped suit in the last year. I wasn't sure Foster would appreciate my help, but what the heck.

I slipped out of the bunny slippers Nat had given me last Christmas and into the flats I'd worn home from work. Where was my bag? I found it and grabbed my same old jacket. It went much better with the paint-spattered jeans than it did with dress-up clothes. Thirty seconds later I was on my way.

No snow yet. I just wished it would start already and get it over with. Even the wind had stopped by the time I neared Cherry Creek Mall. The calm before the storm. I drove into the lot at the back of the cleaners and parked.

Something was wrong. I sensed it even before I climbed out of the van. There seemed to be a black hole in the window above the desk in my office. Usually it reflected the neon lights of the shopping center behind the plant.

I walked over toward the Dumpster that was underneath the window and tripped over a wooden crate that someone hadn't bothered to put inside the big metal container. I cursed under my breath.

As soon as I regained my footing, I took a better look at the window. The glass was broken, and I could see a faint light coming from inside. It was the distant glow from the track lighting I'd left on above the overhead conveyor in the call office, but I shouldn't have been able to see it. I'd closed my office door when I left work that night.

CHAPTER
6

I looked around for a phone to call the police. The only business in the small strip center that would be open this time of night was Tico Taco's, a Mexican restaurant, but it was closed on Mondays. Just my luck this was still Monday, even though it seemed like a couple of weeks since Betty came into the call office with her shopping cart.

I went over to the van, my heart pumping so hard I could hear it in my ears. Damn, I was mad. Mad at whoever had violated my place of business. Mad at myself for not having the window wired into our security system. If I had, an alarm would have gone off at our security company, and the police would have been here already.

David, my insurance man and upcoming date for the Christmas party, had even warned me about the missing link in the security system when I'd renewed my policy last year, but I hadn't gotten around to doing anything about it. Nope, if it was good enough for Uncle Chet, it was good enough for me. He hadn't wired the window because he'd always locked Spot in the office at night and left the window open a crack so Spot could go in and out. Uncle Chet and that damned cat.

I started to turn on the ignition to go find a pay phone when I looked over at the Dumpster again. Betty! I should have thought of her sooner. Hadn't she nearly scared me to death one day last summer when she'd emerged from the Dumpster just as I arrived for work? Whether she'd spent the night inside or was just foraging through it, I didn't know. But wouldn't the cleaners be a logical place for her to come if she was on the run from a killer, not to mention the police?

It was too cold for her to sleep outside tonight, so she could have decided to seek shelter in the plant. Just drag that wooden crate up to the Dumpster, climb on its heavy metal lid, and break out the window. Bingo. She'd be in the cleaners with a nice place to spend the night. I wondered if she'd give me back the twenty dollars to help replace the window she'd broken.

I rummaged around in the back of the van until I found a tire iron. Always have a backup plan of action, just in case your neat little scenario is wrong, I thought. I went over and unlocked the door to the plant.

"Betty. It's me—Mandy," I said in a loud whisper as soon as I stepped inside. "Hey, Betty, come on out— wherever you are."

The light was on above Mack's spotting board, but the place suddenly seemed dark and scary. I switched on the overhead light and started to deactivate the burglar alarm, but as soon as I glanced around, I wasn't so sure Betty was the intruder. She wouldn't hide in here and then start rummaging through the clothes. Or would she? Someone had tipped over a cart full of clothes that Mack had already sorted to go in the dry-cleaning machine the next morning. Other garments were tossed helter-skelter around his work station. Maybe she'd used the clothes as a place to sleep

"Betty," I called again. "Don't be afraid. It's just me, and I need to talk to you."

No answer. The jumble of clothes reminded me of the mess in the closet at O'Brien and Van Dyke. I shuddered and headed for my office to call the police.

The burglar alarm began to wail. A signal would be going to our security company by now, but a call might get the cops here even sooner. And so what if it was Betty? I'd planned to call Foster as soon as I talked to her anyway. I was tired of feeling responsible for her safety. All because of that stupid twenty dollars.

I hurried to my desk, where I could see the phone from the lights out in the plant. I punched in 911. Just as a dispatcher came on the line, I saw my office door move. A dark figure hurtled from behind it and out of the room.

I threw down the phone and took out in pursuit, lugging the tire iron with me. If I'd had time to consider what I was doing, I might have thought better of it. I grabbed a handful of his jacket as the ski-masked burglar ran toward the back door. He strained to get away from me, but I held on to the material, skidding along behind him on our epoxied floor like someone being pulled over ice. I should have worn my Nikes, not the flats with the slippery soles. I couldn't get any traction, and the fabric slipped out of my hand as he wrenched open the door. I took one swing with the tire iron before he sucker punched me in the stomach. The blow packed a wallop that knocked the air out of me. I went sprawling to the floor. The piles of clothes may have softened the fall, but the last of my wind whooshed out as I landed.

By the time I got some air back in my lungs and reached the door, the intruder had disappeared, probably around the side of the building. At least the blow had knocked some sense into me. I didn't attempt to follow him.

I realized I didn't have any idea what I'd have done if I had been able to hold on to the piece of material I'd had in my grasp. It was probably that ripstop nylon used in ski jackets that's so tough I couldn't even rip off a piece as evidence.

"Damn, damn, damn!" The words were punctuated with gasps of air. I slammed the door, locked it, and went back to the phone.

"Hello, hello." I could hear the voice even before I picked up the receiver. Thank God, police dispatchers must be trained to stay on the line even when no one's there.

"This is Mandy Dyer," I puffed, still out of breath from my ill-conceived attempt at bravery. "There's been a break-in at my cleaners and someone just knocked me down." I doubled over to see if that would help me pump up my lungs.

"Is the person still there?" the woman on the other end of the line asked.

"No, he got away." The blare of the alarm continued in the background.

"Are you all right?"

I wanted to scream that, no, I was not all right, that my business had been trashed and I felt as if I were going to throw up. Instead I said, "Yes, I think I'll be okay . . ." I stopped to gulp in some air, and the dispatcher said she'd send someone to the cleaners right away. I gave her the address. "Oh, and have them come to the back of the plant. I'll let them in." I hung up and started to the back door to shut off the alarm.

Halfway there I thought about my computer. It's a thirty-thousand-dollar system, customized to our particular operation with a special program added for the business route. The computer looked all right, but I turned it on and used our password to get into the system. Everything looked okay. No one could get in without the password and an employee number. Still, I was glad I backed up everything on floppies and took them home with me at night.

Whoops. Maybe I shouldn't have touched the computer, in case the police wanted to check for fingerprints, but relief that the computer was okay outweighed guilt at tampering with possible evidence. Besides, the burglar had been wearing gloves. I'd seen one of them when he landed the punch to my stomach.

He could have taken the gloves off inside, I supposed. I went over and looked at the safe but resisted the urge to open it. All I did was take a look. No obvious attempt had been made to break into it, so the only thing left for me to do was pace and wait for the cops. And shut off the burglar alarm. It was driving me crazy.

My breath was coming in short, shallow puffs, and I was still feeling nauseous. The alarm didn't help. I turned it off and went outside to wait, hoping the cold night air would help me regain my breath and settle my queasy stomach.

Snowflakes had finally begun to fall. They stuck in my hair and wet my cheeks. Too bad the snow hadn't started sticking to the ground yet. If it had, the burglar might have left an incriminating trail of footprints going away from the building.

I slid down the wall like one of those melting watches in a Salvador Dali painting. I squatted on the ground until I saw the police car round the building. Then I wondered if I'd be able to get back up.

A uniformed cop got out of the car. "I'm Officer Valdez," he said. "Are you Ms. Dyer?"

I nodded as I rose to my feet.

"I understand there's been a burglary here."

"Someone broke in that window over there." I pointed to the dark hole above my office and explained how the guy had been hiding inside when I tried to call 911.

It had to have been a man. I was sure Betty couldn't have landed such a blow to my midsection, and I didn't want to involve her in the break-in. Still trying to protect the bag lady.

The young policeman was dark and swarthy, but he had kind, serious eyes that looked at me sympathetically. "Are you okay?"

I nodded again, and the cold air had made me feel better.

"Could you give me a description of your assailant?"

When I tried, it was like trying to describe Betty in the Hefty bag. "He wasn't too tall, maybe five-eight or so, a little overweight, and he was dressed in black with a dark ski mask over his head."

Another cop appeared and said he'd begin a search of the neighborhood.

"Was anything stolen?" Valdez asked.

"The safe looks okay, and my computer's all right." Something nagged at me about the description I'd just given him. "But the guy tossed clothes all over the floor as if he'd been looking for something." I led Valdez into the plant and showed him the mess.

"Sounds like a kid, if that's what he did."

I kept thinking of the burglar. The bloody suit could have

fit the guy I'd wrestled with. Suddenly it occurred to me that maybe that's what he'd been looking for—the bloody suit.

I was so excited I almost forgot that my stomach hurt. I told Valdez about Betty and the suit I'd turned over to Stan Foster earlier in the day. Verbalizing it made it seem like the only logical reason someone would break in on this particular night.

My mind was on fast-spin cycle now. "If he came looking for the suit, that means he probably knows about Betty. I wasn't sure about that when I talked to Detective Foster, but the killer could have seen her take it out of the trash can and followed her here."

I bent down and picked up an expensive-looking black cocktail dress with gold threads in it. It had an Oscar de la Renta label on it.

"Oh, God." I dropped it as if I'd been scalded by a shot of steam. "It's torn all the way down the front."

I fell to my knees and started going through other garments on the floor. Valdez bent down beside me.

"Look at this." I showed him a pair of pants. It was ripped down one leg.

A black wool skirt. Torn from waistband to hem. A white silk blouse. It looked as if someone had stabbed it over and over again.

"What kind of nut would do something like this?" It was a rhetorical question. I was sure it was the same person who'd killed Van Dyke.

As I rose to my feet, I grabbed a woman's beige sweater that was a combination of wool and suede. It probably cost three or four hundred dollars. A pair of scissors tumbled out of the sweater and clattered to the floor.

"Where did those come from?" Valdez asked.

"The guy probably got them over there." I motioned to Mack's spotting board. "My dry cleaner uses them to remove loose threads from clothes if the woman who checks them in happens to miss them."

I stared at the scissors. The burglar's instrument of destruction. What he hadn't been able to tear or rip, he'd stabbed or cut in a crazed frenzy of—what?—clothes killing? I was clasping the sweater to me as if it were a living thing, and I finally forced myself to look at it. He'd slit it down the front, and its yarn looked like my nerves felt—all frayed and ready to unravel.

Valdez wanted to check my office where snow was now blowing across my desk. While he inspected the safe, I covered the computer with one of the drop cloths that Mack and the pressers use to keep long dresses from getting dirtied by the floor when they're being worked on.

"No sign of anyone trying to force it," he said, and asked me to open it.

The cash was secure inside. I'd gone to the bank with the day's receipts at four-thirty and placed only the money inside from close-up and for the start of business tomorrow morning.

Valdez insisted that I walk him through the rest of the plant. The only things the burglar could have stolen from up front were clothes, and nothing seemed to be out of place. Besides, the guy hadn't been holding anything as he fought to get away from me.

"It sure looks like something a kid would do," Valdez said when we completed the search. "It's just the kind of malicious mischief some of them are into these days."

I couldn't let him think that way. "Look, if the killer came looking for his bloody suit, he'd want to disguise the reason for the break-in. What better way to do it than to destroy a bunch of clothes?"

Valdez mulled over what I'd said.

"Will you at least tell Detective Foster about the break-in?" I asked. "I'm sure it's connected to the Van Dyke murder."

He nodded, and as long as he'd agreed, I decided there was no need to use my other argument about how the crazed killer had slashed the clothes in frustration and anger when he couldn't find the suit. Had he stabbed at them with the scissors the way he'd stabbed at Van Dyke? It was spooky. I was convinced I'd actually tried to apprehend the killer.

"If he came looking for the suit, that must mean there's something about it that he believes can identify him," I continued as we returned to the cleaning department. "If he's afraid of that, I'm sure he's afraid that Betty can identify him too."

I was about to ask Valdez if he could call Foster and see if the police had turned up any information about her.

Just then the door popped open. With the possible exception of the killer, it was the person I least wanted to see.

Nat Wilcox, ace reporter, had tracked me down. He might be my best friend, but he was the one person I didn't want to know about the bag lady. He'd blab it all over the morning paper, and if the killer didn't know about Betty already, he would by the time Nat got through writing his story.

CHAPTER 7

Nat looked like a cross between a snow-covered spaceman and one of Hell's Angels. What he actually was, though, was Clark Kent without the ability to fly. He insisted on riding his motorcycle, summer or winter, on the theory that it got him to fast-breaking stories quicker than more conventional forms of transportation.

If he was any indication, the storm had turned into a blizzard. Snow was encrusted on his prescription goggles and caked to his jeans and aviator jacket. He looked so pathetic that I almost felt sorry for him. Almost.

"What the hell are you doing here?" I asked. I'd have been glad to see him under other circumstances, but I knew he was wearing his reporter hat tonight.

"Is that any way to treat a friend?" he asked. "I went to your place, and when you didn't show up, I got worried about you. I figured I'd swing by here on my way home."

The plant actually was on the way to his apartment, but I didn't believe for a minute that he'd been worried about me.

He was hunting me down to find out about the evidence I'd turned over to the police.

"So what's going on?" he asked.

Nat can't see worth anything, and he squinted at us until he managed to pull off the wet leather jacket and get his regular wire-rimmed glasses out from where they were hooked over the neck of his NEVER TRUST ANYONE OVER 30 sweatshirt. Nat and I, not to mention the sweatshirt, had crested that hill several years back.

"Someone broke into the plant tonight," I said.

"Did it have something to do with that bloody suit you turned over to the police today?" Trust Nat to hone in on the big story. Somewhere along the way he'd managed to finagle the information out of one of his sources. At least it wasn't me.

Just as long as Officer Valdez didn't mention Betty to him, we were all right. I introduced the two men quickly, stressing the fact that Nat was a reporter. "I'm sorry, but the police told me I couldn't discuss it."

Nat turned to Valdez. "So what happened here?"

Valdez had gotten my message. "A break-in. Appears to be malicious mischief."

"What do you mean, malicious mischief?"

I interrupted. "Someone came in and destroyed some clothes. Okay? Nothing stolen or anything."

"Ms. Dyer here tried to apprehend the suspect, but he got away," Valdez said.

Nat looked over at me quickly. "You all right?"

I nodded, even though my stomach was probably going to be so sore tomorrow I'd feel as if I'd scrimmaged with the Denver Broncos.

Valdez asked what I wanted to do about the window, call

someone out on overtime to replace it or board it up temporarily. With Nat's help we nailed some wood over it until morning. It didn't make my office any warmer, but it kept the snow from blowing in.

After assuring himself that I had a way home, Valdez took the scissors and left. He'd wanted to take the clothes, too, in case the police apprehended the burglar and needed the garments for evidence; however, he agreed to pick them up the next day so I'd have a chance to assess the damage and find out who the owners were.

Nat insisted on hanging around. I went back to the office and removed the snow-covered drop cloth from my desk.

"So do you want to go out for coffee?" Nat asked.

"No, I need to figure out how much damage there is." By then Nat had seen the shredded clothes.

"I'll help."

"It may take a while."

Nat followed me out to the cleaning department. "That's okay. I don't think you ought to be here alone."

Sure, like I was going to believe that.

I looked at the poor, bedraggled guy and softened. "Well, if you're going to stay, you'd better get out of those wet clothes." It was the least I could do to make up for the lie I was about to tell him.

I went over by the boiler room and dug through a box until I found a pair of sweats for him to put on. They were green with red trim at the neck. I also found a pair of heavy wool socks.

"Here." I tossed them to him. "They're from our Christmas drive for the homeless shelters, and we've already cleaned them." I was pleased with myself, because this also laid the groundwork for the story I was going to tell him about the bloody suit.

I swooped up his leather jacket from the floor and hung it on a hanger. "This may shrink. You ought to let me send it to our leather cleaner."

Nat declined and asked if he could bring his Harley inside. I wasn't surprised. He takes a lot better care of his Hog than he does of himself or his clothes. In fact as a customer he's the pits because he favors non-dry-cleanable apparel, such as stone-washed jeans and drip-dry shirts.

"Okay, bring the infernal thing in," I said. After all, if the floor was designed to withstand, God forbid, a chemical spill, what would a little snow do.

He grinned at me and hauled in the cycle, which by now looked like a conveyance suitable only for the Abominable Snowman. Then he went to the rest room to change his clothes.

Nat and I used to see eye to eye on things when we were back in high school. Physically as well as philosophically. We'd both been about five foot five at age sixteen, but I stopped growing. Nat managed to eke out a few more inches and is probably about the same height as the owner of the bloody suit. Only difference is he's skinny and looks a little like John Lennon. It's a look he cultivates by wearing the granny glasses and letting his dark hair grow longer than the current fashion.

Philosophically we'd wanted to make a better world back in high school, but now we sometimes argued about his need to go into all the gory details of a story. Sensationalism just to sell papers, I said. The public's right to know, he maintained.

"I'm glad you didn't get hurt tonight," he said when he

returned from the rest room, all decked out like one of Santa's helpers. And he really did pitch in and help.

He cleaned up the glass in my office while I checked out the clothes. Altogether I found about two dozen garments that had been damaged in the burglar's onslaught. Not as many as I'd feared. Probably I'd interrupted the guy in his rampage, or the whole plant would have been torn apart.

It took me a while longer to match up the tag numbers on the garments, which Nat called out to me, with the tickets that identified the customers who'd brought in the clothes. Without the computer it would have taken much longer. As it was, we were both freezing by the time I shut off the computer and led Nat out of my office.

I heated up some leftover coffee in a pot in the employee break room and offered Nat a cup. I knew he didn't mind. Nat would drink coffee cold, thick as mud, or weak as water.

"Okay, what's the scoop?" he asked. "Now that I've helped you out, come clean with me, Mandy." He sounded like my answering-machine message. "Where'd you get the suit?"

I sat down on the old leather sofa we had in the break room. "All right, but it'll have to be off the record for now."

Nat sat in one of the chairs at the Formica-topped table. "Oh, come off it, Mandy."

"No, the police don't want me to talk about it."

"Okay, okay. It's off the record." I wondered if he was crossing his fingers behind his back where I couldn't see them.

"And in return you'll have to tell me what you know about the case."

He shrugged. "Fine. You first."

"No, you first."

We sounded like the thirteen-year-old kids we'd been when we first met in Mrs. Henderson's English class.

"So what do you want to know?" Nat asked. I figured he was being so agreeable because he really wanted my information. "Van Dyke was stabbed. Slashed is more like it. Over and over, like someone had completely flipped out."

"I already know that." Just like the person who'd stabbed the clothes. "So when do the police think Van Dyke was killed?"

"Maybe five or six o'clock this morning. He hadn't been dead long when his secretary found him."

Too bad. I'd kind of hoped the murder had happened earlier. This way, Betty definitely could have been making her rounds and been seen by the killer when she retrieved the suit from the trash can.

"Your turn, Mandy," Nat said. "Where'd you find the suit?"

I hoped I didn't start to itch. I used to get so nervous when I lied that all my nerve endings began to tingle. In fact Nat swore we'd have gotten away with cutting class in eighth grade if I hadn't begun to scratch when I told Mrs. Henderson how Nat and I had been attacked by a mugger who stole our book reports on the way to school.

"Remember those clothes I told you about that we're cleaning for the homeless shelters for Christmas?" I said. "The suit was in the donation box."

Nat had taken off his glasses to clean them, and he couldn't see me all that well. Otherwise I'm sure he'd have known I was lying, especially when I feigned a sneeze so I could scratch my nose.

"Why is that off the record, for Christ's sake?"

"Just until I check it out with Detective Foster."

Funny, how I'd trust Nat with all my personal problems and not with the information for a story. I figured he'd respect his off-the-record promise if it was something dull like finding the suit in a collection box. I wasn't sure he was strong enough to resist writing about Betty.

He put his glasses back on. "Where was the collection box?"

"Uh—here at the store. Well, we left the box outside for a while so people could drop clothes in it at night." My hair follicles were beginning to tickle, so I ran my hands through my hair as casually as I could. "But we didn't do it tonight because of the storm."

"Hmmm."

I was afraid he was getting suspicious, so I gave him something to nibble on. "I went over to O'Brien and Van Dyke this morning because the police wanted me to take a look at the closet we use for our delivery service." No need to tell him I was the one who talked Detective Foster into letting me go. "The killer must have seen me there or found out about it and got so nervous he came here looking for the suit."

Nat mulled that over, and actually it could have happened that way, come to think of it. Me with the Dyer's Cleaners logo emblazoned on my jacket. I might as well have had on a flashing neon sign, but at least maybe that meant the killer didn't know about Betty.

"What are you thinking?" Nat asked.

Actually I was thinking about how I'd offered to draw a sketch of the bag lady right there in the law firm's reception area. Foster'd had to drag me away from Ms. Sexy Voice's desk. Me and my big mouth.

"Come on," Nat said. "What's on your mind?"

I grappled with something else I could be thinking about. "I was wondering if they've arrested anyone yet."

"No, but there was apparently a big fight at the law firm Friday night. Harrison Van Dyke, the guy who was killed, got in a real screaming match with his partner, Frank O'Brien, and Van Dyke's son."

"Vance?" I asked.

"Yeah, how'd you know the son's name?"

"We try to know all our customers by name."

"Well, I guess you're not apt to forget a name like Vance Van Dyke, are you?"

"So how'd you find out about the fight?"

"I have my sources." Nat smiled mysteriously, like a nearsighted Mona Lisa.

"What was it about?"

"I haven't been able to find out yet, but I will."

"So what else did you discover?"

"That O'Brien was Van Dyke's father-in-law."

"That's interesting." I thought about it for a minute. "One time right after Uncle Chet died, Mr. O'Brien was in here, and he said he thought it was great that I'd taken over the business. He said he wished he'd taught his daughter something about business so she'd be more self-sufficient. He must have been referring to Mrs. Van Dyke."

O'Brien was an elderly man with a few wispy hairs on top of his head. He made me think of words like courtly and Kewpie doll. He wasn't too tall, and he had a paunch, which meant he could probably wear the bloody suit. Still, I couldn't see him stabbing Van Dyke to death or having the strength to break into the plant, much less deliver me a knockdown blow.

When I looked over, Nat had taken out his notebook. It

reminded me of Foster, but with Nat the notebook was almost like an appendage to his right arm. Normally, however, he didn't have it out when he was talking to me.

"I have to get some sleep, Nat, so we're going to have to get out of here."

"Don't you want to stay and guard the place? I could stay with you if you want." As he made the offer, I could see him looking at the couch possessively.

I glanced at my watch. It was already two A.M., and I wanted to make sure I was here when—or if—Betty arrived. "I guess we could, providing you're willing to sleep on the floor. I think there are even a couple of sleeping bags around here that no one ever claimed."

He agreed, and I got the bags. I tossed him one, and turned off the light on my way to the couch. Once I climbed into the sleeping bag, I asked casually, "How do you like Stan Foster?"

"He's okay. Pretty much a by-the-book kind of cop. Why do you ask?"

"I think he's sexy-looking."

In the faint light from the call office where the track lighting was still on above the overhead conveyor, I could see Nat sit up, like a mummy rising from the tomb.

"Haven't you learned your lesson about those tall, handsome guys?" Of course he was referring to Larry the Law Student, whom he'd warned me not to marry.

"You should talk. What about you and all those tall, willowy blondes you're always attracted to? How's Suzanne, by the way?"

Nat slunk back down in the mummy bag. "She dumped me."

"What was the reason this time?"

"We were on our way to the Bronco game when I picked up this police chase on the scanner. . . ."

I got up on one elbow. "And you took off in hot pursuit, no doubt."

"Yeah, but I found her a ride back to Denver when the guy finally cracked up his car outside of Colorado Springs."

"That's seventy miles away, Nat."

"You're a fine one to talk. That actor you dated wasn't very happy when you missed his gala opening because you had to clean football uniforms all night."

I lay back down again. "Well, the kids couldn't very well play football with that Gatorade that got spilled all over them."

"Right."

Sometimes I wondered if Nat and I were the only people of the opposite sex who could stand each other. On rare occasions I even wondered what it would be like to go to bed with him. But I didn't think about it for long because I didn't want to risk our friendship for a few minutes of sex, which might or might not be any good. Of course our friendship might be over anyway, once he found out about Betty the Bag Lady.

"Hey, Mandy, remember the time you ran away from home and were sleeping at Chet's old store downtown?"

I could feel myself drifting off to sleep. "Yeah, why?"

"This reminds me of the night I came down to stay with you because you were scared of being in the plant alone."

"Oh, yeah, the night McKenzie discovered our hiding place." I'd forgotten about being scared inside the plant back then. I thought tonight was the first time.

"My old man beat the hell out of me when I got home," Nat said.

I roused up. "I never knew that."

He didn't answer. I wasn't sure if he'd fallen asleep or just didn't want to talk about it anymore. I'd always known his dad beat him. I just didn't know he'd done it because of me.

"This is off the record," Nat said.

I thought maybe he was going to tell me something more about his father.

"The police are keeping it quiet, but they say Van Dyke was covered with an Indian blanket when his secretary found the body."

I tried to think about the significance of one of those Navajo rugs from the law firm's walls being thrown over the body, but all I could think of was Nat's father.

"About that donation box," Nat continued. "Did you see anyone who could have put the suit in it?"

"No, it must have been left there just before we got to work." I couldn't control myself anymore. I had to sit up and scratch. "These sleeping bags sure make you itch, don't they?"

Now I couldn't get back to sleep. I felt sad and guilty. I wasn't sure if it was about Nat's father, my lie to him, or the fact that Betty was out there in the raging storm somewhere. I could hear the wind whistle through the boarded-up window in my office next to the break room.

When I finally dozed off, I had nightmares. In one I was running after Betty, trying to save her, while a faceless man in a bloody suit pursued us both. We ran inside the cleaners and locked the door. The man began to beat on the door, breaking it down.

I bolted upright from the sleeping bag, wet with perspiration. I still heard the noises.

I'd thought it was ridiculous when Nat said we should

stick around and guard the place because the intruder might come back again. I was wrong.

The banging came again. No mistaking it this time. Only it didn't sound like someone banging on the door. It sounded as if the person was just outside the break room by the cleaning machines.

CHAPTER
8

I crawled out of the sleeping bag and shook Nat. He mumbled something and rolled over. So much for having backup. I tiptoed out of the break room to a position beside one of the cleaning machines. I took a quick look around the corner of the machine.

A big, dark figure was stomping his feet. I jerked my head back before he saw me, then out again to take a better look.

"Mack," I yelled. "What are you doing here?"

The poor guy jumped a foot. He'd have gotten an award for overacting if he'd been onstage.

"My God, is that you, Mandy? What do you mean, scaring me that way?" He turned on the lights and stooped to retrieve a big box of doughnuts he'd dropped on the floor.

I came out of my hiding place. "What time is it, anyway?"

"Quarter to seven." He picked up the box. Fortunately the doughnuts hadn't spilled on the floor.

"Oh, Jeez. I haven't turned up the boiler yet."

Mack and I took turns tending to the boiler so the pressers

would have steam when they came to work. This week it was my turn, and I'd almost blown it.

"I wondered about that when I came in. I saw the van, but there were no lights except up front." Mack finished stomping the snow off his galoshes, which was the chore I'd interrupted with my cloak-and-dagger routine. He was wearing a navy pea jacket and a black knit cap, and he looked like the burglar, only larger. More like an aging sailor on shore leave in a place he didn't want to be. Try Siberia, from the looks of him.

"There was a break-in here last night," I said.

He quit brushing snow off his shoulders, and his eyes darted around the place, then back at me. "Are you all right?"

I told him I was, then launched into the story about the slashed clothes and my theory that Van Dyke's killer had seen Betty grab his bloody suit out of the trash can, followed her here, and come back during the night to try to find the suit.

I went over and turned on the overhead lights and showed him the clothes. He shook his head sadly. We dry cleaners are like that when anything is ruined.

"Or," Mack pointed out, "he could have come here because you went over to the law firm, all decked out like a Christmas tree in your Dyer's Cleaners jacket."

"My second choice," I said, but sometime during the night I'd decided it probably wasn't my trip to the law firm that had precipitated the break-in. The killer surely would have known I'd turned the suit over to the police when he saw me there with Detective Foster.

"You should have called me," Mack said. "What'd you do—stay here all night to clean up the mess?"

Just then Nat appeared to see what all the commotion was. He looked as disheveled as I felt.

"What's he doing here?" Mack apparently hadn't yet noticed the motorcycle by the door.

"Nat stayed here with me to guard the place."

"Some help he'd be. He didn't even wake up when I came in."

Nat yawned.

Mack looked disapproving. You'd have thought we were still teenagers rather than consenting adults, and the part no one would ever believe was that we hadn't done anything either time we'd spent the night together.

Mack had always had this protective attitude about me. When he'd found Nat and me hiding out in the old plant, he'd called our parents. It was right after Mom's fourth marriage, and my new stepfather grounded me for a month.

But Mack is also the person who mourned Uncle Chet's death with me and convinced me I could run the cleaners myself. Since Larry had just left me, I needed the moral support. Uncle Chet's wife, Emily, had died years before, and my mother was no help. She was too upset about my breakup with Larry. Nat of course didn't want me to take over the cleaners and give up my dream of being artist.

"I could have been down here in ten minutes if you'd just called," Mack grumbled as he tromped past Nat into the break room with the doughnuts.

I told him he could still help me by getting the boiler turned up. Then I grabbed Nat's jeans out of the dryer, tossed them to him so he could change, and sent him and his Harley on their way.

By the time the rest of the crew arrived for work, it was

business as usual—except for my vigil at the back door waiting for Betty to appear.

I interspersed my nervous sentry duty with other things I had to do.

First, I grabbed one of my freshly pressed suits and a blouse from the conveyor. I found a new pair of panty hose in a desk drawer in my office and adjourned to the rest room to change out of the jeans and sweatshirt I'd worn when I came down to the plant the night before.

That's one of the nice things about owning a cleaners. You get your clothes cleaned free, and there's always something to wear hanging around the plant, not to mention unclaimed sleeping bags and used clothing to loan to friends.

The outfit I happened to have available today was a black skirt and a long gold jacket with a black-and-white-striped blouse. I shimmied into the panty hose, which was the main thing I hated about dressing up. By the time I put on the suit and slipped back into my pair of flats, no one would have guessed that I'd spent the night "crashing" in the office with Nat.

Oh, yeah? I looked at myself in the mirror. My short dark hair was standing on end. No lovable tousled look here. Definitely punk rocker. I combed my hair, washed my mouth out with Listerine, and put on some lipstick. That was the best I could do. I needed something to cover the circles under my eyes and remove the knot from my stomach. They'd have to wait for another day, although the knot might take longer. I'd noticed as I dressed that there was a bruise on my midsection where the burglar had punched me.

By nine o'clock I'd already gotten the glass company out

to replace the window, made an appointment with the security company to hook my office window into our burglar alarm system, and left a message for David Withers to call me about filing an insurance claim. Oh, please, let the insurance cover the losses despite the stupid window.

I made one more trip to the back door. "Betty really should have been here by now," I said to Mack, who was at the spotting table nearby.

He turned to me with a spray gun as if he were about to squirt it at me. "Will you quit coming back here every five minutes? You're getting on my nerves. You wouldn't want me to ruin this wedding gown, would you?"

He held up a handful of satin. I could see wine mixed in with the seed pearls on the bodice of the gown, and no, I wouldn't want him to ruin it. Once we had it cleaned, we'd box it up in what we called our "Keepsake" packaging and charge about $250 for our work.

I started to walk away, then stopped. "She's usually here by this time, isn't she?"

Mack nodded. "But some people are smarter than the rest of us. They don't go out in this kind of weather. She usually doesn't come around in a blizzard. Now, will you just scat."

I tried to figure out how best to utilize my time. As soon as the glass man finished installing the window, I could reclaim my office and do the research I'd planned to do the night before: make a list of the O'Brien and Van Dyke customers who'd sent us gray-pinstriped suits within the last year.

Meanwhile business would be so slow today because of the storm that I didn't need to work at the front counter. Maybe I'd run a spot check on the clothes at packaging. I do that occasionally, just to see if everything's up to our standards.

As soon as I decided what to do, someone pounded on the back door. I was sure it was Betty, despite Mack's predictions to the contrary. I ran over and opened the door, letting in a blast of arctic wind and a swirl of snowflakes.

It was the glass man. I'd thought he was still in my office. He had on a cap with earflaps and looked like a frozen basset hound. "Got the window back in," he said. "Just had to go out to the truck to get the paperwork for you to sign."

I thanked him, signed my name, and watched him as he went back to his truck. Actually I was looking for Betty. All I saw was about a foot of snow.

The frigid air sent a chill through my body. Strange that I could be so cold and still feel like a malfunctioning boiler, its contents under pressure and ready to explode at any minute. God, I wished Betty would show up so I would quit having this picture of her dead in some alley.

"Will you shut that damned door?" Mack said. "It's getting cold in here."

I closed the door, remembering the first real conversation I'd had with Betty. It had been much different from today. One of those summer mornings when I yearned to escape to the mountains with my sketch pad. I was standing outside the back door, having a cup of coffee and thinking about playing hooky. I'd heard her coming with her squeaky shopping cart, and by the time she got there, I was ready with a doughnut and a cup of coffee for her.

We stood there for a few minutes while she polished off the doughnut. "This is just like 'avin' tea and crumpets with Princess Di," she said, feigning a British accent that made Cockney sound good. " 'Cept in your case, the Di's for Dyer, not Diana." She wheeled her cart away, chuckling over her own cleverness.

After that she'd always say, "Thanks for the tea and crumpets, Princess Di," if I were at the door when she showed up. Finally I handed her some hot water and a tea bag, and she looked at me as if I'd gone completely daft.

"Getting even with me, are ye, mum?" she'd said, and told me in no uncertain terms what she thought of tea. "It makes me mouth shrivel up like I been eatin' walnuts."

"So where are you *really* from?" I asked her. "I know you're not from England, or you'd like tea."

"Where I'm from ain't polite to talk about in 'igh society, Princess." She scurried away.

It piqued my curiosity, and from then on I always tried to trick her into revealing something about her past. It was a game we played, and one I always lost.

Mack glared at me from the spotting table, interrupting my thoughts. "If Betty shows up, I promise I'll hog-tie her and come get you."

"Thanks," I said, "and by the way, I didn't call Nat last night. He showed up on his own, and I couldn't get rid of him."

Mack didn't say anything, but I was sure that would make him feel better.

When I got to my office, I removed the drop cloth that I'd used to cover the desk again while the window was being replaced. I sat down at the computer and went to the business-route files.

As I'd told Officer Valdez, the killer must think there was some way he could be tied to the bloody suit. Why else would he risk breaking in here? So maybe that meant my plan to check the computer wasn't such a bad idea.

The computer provides a history of all our customers— what kind of garments they send us, the frequency of their visits. If someone comes in asking about a lost garment, we can tell him when he had it cleaned and if and when he picked it up. When customers don't pay us a visit in a predetermined length of time, we can also pull up their names and send them mailers, offering a discount the next time they bring their cleaning to us.

I input the name of O'Brien and Van Dyke. Every customer at the law firm who had sent cleaning to us came up on the computer screen. All the names were cross-referenced, and I could go to each person's individual file, whether he'd sent in orders from the office or come to the plant.

Of course the computer was only as detailed as the input from the people feeding it information, and at a cleaners we didn't care about the label on a suit or the size. Too bad. I wasn't going to be able to look at the garments and find a JCPenney special or a size, but I could go to each name and see who among the O'Brien–Van Dyke employees had sent us a suit—2PC GRAY STRIPE. We don't actually have a key for "pinstripe," so this was what we used to separate it from solid gray.

A lot of people at the law firm had suits that matched the general description. Looking for a gray pinstripe among lawyers, I discovered, was like looking for a pair of blue jeans at a high school.

There was a "gray stripe" for Frank O'Brien, Van Dyke's partner and, according to Nat, his father-in-law. Maybe the hairs on the bloody suit had been white, not blond or light brown. And of course, there was also the fight that Nat had heard about between him and his son-and-law.

Another candidate was Van Dyke's son, who'd also been in on the argument. And a name like Vance Van Dyke might be reason to kill, in and of itself, if his father had named him that. Unfortunately Vance was a route customer only; I'd never seen him.

Another person with a gray pinstripe was Eric Jenkins, the cocky bantam rooster who'd been talking to David outside the cleaners yesterday morning. His waistline might have been larger before he began pumping iron, which could have accounted for the pulled fabric at the button.

I soon had a list of eight names. None for Jake Benson. The trouble was that the owners of the suits could be tall, short, fat, or thin. I didn't know. And I didn't ignore the women either. After all, they sometimes sent in items for their husbands, and if Van Dyke had been fooling around with one of the women in the office, maybe an irate husband had killed him. I took special note of Pamela Leyton, Ms. Sexy Voice, but actually I didn't find any more candidates.

The most likely person on the list, according to my clothing profile, was Eric, who'd been a regular customer of Dyer's Cleaners since long before we started the route service. I put a star by his name because he was the one person I knew who'd been at the cleaners around the same time as Betty. He could have followed her here, and he was about the right height for the suit. Even better, he had light brown hair that could be a match for the loose hairs on the suit jacket. And he was one of those lawyers who thought he was "the cat's pajamas," as Uncle Chet used to say about Larry the Law Student while at the same time covering his interest in both cats and clothes.

I wondered if Eric smoked. It didn't seem likely, considering the fact that he was a bodybuilder, but you couldn't tell about people, and I mustn't ignore the cigarette burn and the dandruff on the suit, even though Detective Foster had refused to let me share that information with him.

Back in the days when Dashiell Hammett and Raymond Chandler were writing detective stories, a cigarette burn might not have been a significant clue, but now that we were a nonsmoking society, it could be significant. Even Uncle Chet had been quick to make the cleaners a nonsmoking environment when he moved to the new plant, and in fact I finally broke the habit myself when I took over the business.

Just out of curiosity I started to pull up Harrison Van Dyke's name on the computer when Julia, one of my morning counter people, knocked on the door. Despite my open-door policy, I'd kept the door shut this morning until it warmed up in the office.

"You know, you really need to get an intercom, Mandy," she said.

Yeah, yeah, as soon as I buy about a hundred other things we need, plus pay the claims on all the ruined clothes.

"I get tired of walking all the way back here every time someone wants to talk to you," Julia said. "Anyway, Eric Jenkins is out front and wants to see you."

Well, speak of the devil.

CHAPTER 9

Normally I want to see Eric about as much as I want to see a customer with a complaint that we've ruined a three-thousand-dollar designer original. Who wants to listen to his bumper-sticker slogans about how "Lawyers Do It at Sidebar" and "Cleaners Do It Dirty"?

But today curiosity won out over good taste. I followed Julia to the front counter. She's an overworked mother of three, which probably accounts for why she hates to run back and forth to my office with messages.

"Do you want to take a break?" I asked as I caught up with her. "I'll take over at the counter for a while." She was only too happy to detour to the break room.

I reached the call office. Ann Marie had just finished with another customer and was heading for Eric.

"Boy, that's a neat car you got," she said with a teenager's enthusiasm as she looked outside at his flashy red BMW. "Bet it goes real fast, huh?"

I looked out, unimpressed by the car but relieved to see that the snow had finally quit.

"Why don't you go back and help Lucille bag some garments for a while, Ann Marie?" I asked.

She went bouncing off angrily, like a yo-yo on a short string.

"Hi, Eric. What did you want to see me about?"

He was all business. "I have a suit that was supposed to be delivered to the office today, but under the circumstances I thought you might not be able to make your Tuesday delivery. I decided I'd better pick it up."

He was probably right about the delivery, and I went to the door and asked Ann Marie to retrieve his order from our delivery rack at the back of the plant.

She gave me a dirty look.

While we waited for her to return, I was hoping to find out what Eric *really* wanted. After all, he hadn't needed to talk to me in order to pick up the suit.

"That was really a shock about Mr. Van Dyke," I said when I returned to the counter.

"Yeah," he agreed. "I noticed you over there yesterday morning. What was going on?"

I told him I couldn't discuss it.

"Oh, come on, Mandy, I'll treat it like privileged information between a lawyer and a client."

"Sure."

Eric leaned toward me conspiratorially. "Actually I'm surprised something didn't happen to Harrison long before this, the way he was always hitting on all the women in the office."

"Oh, really?" I wondered if Eric was offering up this bit of gossip in hopes I'd do the same.

"Sure." Eric lowered his voice. "Harrison had this fetish

for Navajo rugs. The rumor was that he used to bed down all the female employees on them. You know what I mean?"

Yuck. And to think that Van Dyke's sole trip into the cleaners had been to inquire about us cleaning his rugs. I'd told him that Navajo rugs shouldn't be cleaned in solvent. It takes out the lanolin. They are best cleaned by taking them outside after a winter storm and rubbing them with snow. That's what an Indian had told me once, but in lieu of that I said we could clean them by hand. He never got around to bringing them to us.

Eric stood back to watch my reaction to his news about the rugs. If true, it might explain what Nat had heard about a Navajo rug being tossed over the body. Some crazed husband or boyfriend could have killed Van Dyke and thrown the rug over him in a jealous rage.

I tried for a wide-eyed look. "Who?" I asked.

"Who what?"

"Who was he sleeping with?"

Just then Ann Marie came out of the back of the plant as if she were about to lead us in a school cheer.

"Here's your order," she said, hooking the suit over the stainless steel rail at the counter. "How much does a car like that cost?"

I could tell she planned to hang around. "Thanks, Ann Marie. You were helping Lucille, weren't you?" She flounced out of the room.

Eric changed the subject. "That detective was asking what clothes I'd left in the closet for you to pick up today. Any idea what that was about?"

I shook my head and went back to the main subject. "So who was Mr. Van Dyke sleeping with?"

Eric apparently decided he'd said too much already, and

since he wasn't getting the information he wanted from me, he grabbed his order and started to leave.

Lord, if he were the killer, maybe he'd even snatched something out of his own bag and was afraid the police would find out about it. That gave me an idea.

"Just a minute," I said. "I'll put this on your monthly bill, but I'll need your ticket." It was stapled to the bag, but it wasn't really necessary that I have it.

I grabbed a furtive look down inside our plastic garment bag. It was the same look I imagined Eric might sneak as he looked down the front of Ms. Sexy Voice's décolletage. Only thing was I simply wanted to check the label on his suit.

Armani. The label one of the customers yesterday morning had guessed would be on the bloody suit but wasn't. The Rolls-Royce of suits. I hadn't known he had that much taste. He probably wasn't the type of guy who'd wear a five-year-old suit from Penney any more than the driver of a Rolls would be happy in an old VW bug.

But it gave me another idea. I should check the rest of the clothes bound for delivery to O'Brien and Van Dyke's offices. I could see if any of the other garments fit the clothing profile I'd developed for the owner of the bloody suit.

Eric seemed to be getting nervous as I labored to remove the staple from the bag. "Hey, don't mention what I just said about the rugs. Okay? It's strictly between you and me."

"I'll treat it as privileged information between a dry cleaner and her customer." I smiled demurely. "We dry cleaners can be very discreet."

Not discreet enough apparently. Eric grabbed his clothes and started to leave.

I stopped him. "You don't smoke, do you?"

"Why do you ask that?"

"My cleaner-spotter thought he saw a cigarette burn on your suit."

"Shit. Where was it?"

He brought the suit back and hung it on the rail.

I lifted the poly bag from the suit. "Here on the lapel." I squinted as if trying to detect the burn. "Hmmm. I don't see it. Mack must have been able to get it out, so it couldn't have been a burn."

"Thank God." Relief made him revert to form. "To tell you the truth, I have a drag once in a while." He lifted one eyebrow suggestively. "But only naked. You know, after sex."

I wasn't sure I needed that much information, but at least I'd found out that he smoked sometimes.

When Julia returned, I left her to handle the counter and went back to the rails that held the work to be delivered this afternoon when our driver came in. It was across from Mack's station.

"No sign of Betty, huh?" I asked.

Mack shook his head.

I found a suit that we'd cleaned for Van Dyke's father-in-law. It was a Brooks Brothers. The senior partner was neither a Rolls nor a VW man. If his suit were a car, I'd say it was a Buick. Unfortunately I couldn't find a size on it, but from eyeballing it, I could see it was about the same size as the bloody suit, maybe just a little smaller.

"What you doing nosin' around in that stuff?" Mack asked.

"Just looking to see if we misplaced an order."

Mack probably didn't buy it, and speaking of nosing around, my nose was beginning to itch from all the lies I'd been telling.

Van Dyke's son didn't have anything on the rail, and I was looking to see what other names I recognized from the list I'd just made off the computer.

Julia interrupted me again just as I came across an order for Harrison Van Dyke himself.

"I don't know how much more of this running back and forth I'm going to be able to handle," she said. "I took the kids to see Santa Claus last night, and I'm so tired, I feel like I'm ready to collapse."

I'd have to make it up to Julia and Ann Marie when this was over. Something extra in their Christmas stocking.

"It's David Withers now," she said. "He wants to see you."

I kept hoping it would be Detective Foster, especially after the break-in last night, and I wasn't looking forward to seeing David. He was probably going to tell me my insurance wouldn't pay our claim because of my inadequate security system.

Actually I think the alarm system only reduced the premiums I paid, and being the responsible businesswoman I am, I went out front to see him.

David had exchanged his jogging suit of yesterday morning for gray slacks and a tweed sports jacket with a pocket protector that said Acme Insurance. At least he didn't look like the tan man now that he was wearing a blue shirt and red and blue tie. He carried a clipboard with a claim form on it.

"I just need to take a look at the damage," he said. "Was anything stolen?"

I shook my head and began to walk him through the plant. "Nothing that I can find, but whoever it was destroyed some clothes back in the dry-cleaning department. I made a list of the garments."

"Does this have something to do with that woman who brought in the suit yesterday?"

"Maybe, but I'd already turned the suit over to the police."

I showed him the clothes, which I'd piled in a basket near Mack's work station, ready for Officer Valdez to pick up. I went to my office to get David the list I'd made up of the damaged clothes.

"How'd they break in?" he asked when I returned.

I took a deep breath. "Through the window in my office."

He apparently didn't remember telling me I ought to have it connected to our security system.

I waited for him to say something, but I finally blurted out a confession. "I never did have it hooked up to the burglar alarm last winter, but the security people are coming out today to take care of it."

He looked up from the clipboard where he'd been trans-ferring the items on my list to his claim form. "Kind of like locking the barn door after the clotheshorse is stolen, huh?"

I groaned. "That's bad, David."

He gave me a lopsided grin. "Just a little insurance humor."

"Do you think Acme will pay the claims?" I asked while I had him in a good mood.

"I'll do my best, and while I'm here, I wanted to confirm about that Christmas party Friday night."

I nodded in relief.

"There's a cash bar starting at six-thirty," he said, "and the dinner is at—"

He never got a chance to finish.

Ann Marie interrupted us, and I was glad Julie hadn't had to walk back here a third time to find me. "That policeman is up front, and he said he needs to talk to you."

This time I asked her to send him to my office. "It may be a while," I said to David.

"No problem, I need to complete the form and take a look at the clothes."

"I still think that cop is a hunk," Ann Marie whispered in my ear as I left David.

By the time Foster got to the office, I was seated behind my desk, ready with my sketch and the list of gray pin-stripes we'd cleaned for members of the law firm.

Foster was carrying a paper sack when he came in, and for a second I was afraid it was all that was left of Betty.

"Well, did the bag lady show up this morning?" he asked.

I shook my head, but at least he hadn't found the grocery sack beside her frozen body.

"I gather that means you didn't find her yesterday," I said.

"No, we haven't been able to locate her."

"She didn't stop by here this morning either."

"I was afraid of that." He shook his head, probably thinking of the twenty dollars I'd been foolish enough to give her yesterday. "I got the report about the break-in here last night."

"I think the person was looking for the suit," I said, "which probably means he knows Betty brought it here. He must have followed her here, or else he overheard us talking about it over at the law firm."

"All the more reason we need to find her."

I reached in my purse and pulled out the sketch of Betty.

He took a long look at it. "Well, at least it looks like a real person."

Faint praise was better than none, I supposed.

"Did your crime lab find out if it was Mr. Van Dyke's blood on the suit?" I asked.

"We don't have the results yet."

And if he did, I figured he wasn't going to tell me about them. But I'd already made my own determination that it was Van Dyke's blood on the suit, and I was proceeding accordingly.

"I made a list of all the people at the law firm who've sent us gray pinstripes in the last year."

"You keep that kind of information?"

I explained to him about the capabilities of our computer but how it didn't show sizes or makes of clothing.

He took the list along with the sketch and made motions to leave. "Oh, by the way, remember how you thought the killer might have stolen something to wear from your dry-cleaning closet. We've talked to your customers, and none of them think any of their clothes are missing from the closet."

"I warned you that lots of people can't remember what they send us."

"In fact," Foster continued, "they can't identify half the clothes that were left on the floor."

"I'm not surprised."

"Well, frankly I find it a little hard to believe." He unfolded himself from the chair.

"Incidentally we have a regular pickup and delivery scheduled at the law firm today," I said. "Are we going to be able to get in yet?"

He was halfway out the door by then, the brown paper

sack still under his arm. "No, we're still going to be there today."

"What's in the sack?" I asked.

He looked at it in surprise. "Oh, yeah, I almost forgot." He thumped the flat of his hand against his forehead. "You know, what you said about getting the ink stains out of shirt pockets."

"Yes." I was puzzled at how the guy could be the efficient professional one minute and an inept private person the next. It was not without appeal.

"Well, I brought in some of my shirts—as long as you said you could do such a good job on them."

I took the sack. "How many shirts?"

"Uh—I didn't count them."

I smiled in satisfaction. "See, and you didn't believe that people over at O'Brien and Van Dyke could forget what they sent us."

He grinned sheepishly. "Okay, you win."

I turned on the computer. "I'll need your home phone number. We use it as your account number."

He reeled it off for me.

There were several other reasons to have a customer's phone number: in case we had a problem cleaning a garment, if the customer forgot to pick it up, or maybe if I ever got up the nerve to ask a customer for a date.

This was the first time I'd ever thought of that final reason, but despite Nat's warning about those tall, handsome guys, I agreed with Ann Marie's assessment of Foster. Nat probably would think David was more my type—safe, sensible, and with a sense of humor. Okay, so the humor wasn't so great, if the remark about a clotheshorse was an example, but it takes a while to get it back after a divorce. I ought to know.

I asked Foster if he could find his own way out this time, and hurried back to where I'd left David. Someone let out a wolf whistle as Foster made his way to the call office. I'd bet it was Ingrid, my silk presser, and I'd have to think about reprimanding her for it, but not now.

"David had to leave," Mack said when I reached the cleaning department, where he was unloading one of the machines. "He said he'd give you a call later and to let him know if you found anything else that was damaged."

I stood there watching Mack and thinking. "Did Betty ever say where she spent her nights when it got cold?"

Mack thought about it for a minute. "She said once that the Capitol Hill Mission had the best digs in town."

"Thanks, Mack." I turned away before he could see the smile on my face. Actor that he was, he could always read me like a bad script. I wouldn't want him to know that I'd decided to stake out the homeless shelter that night.

CHAPTER 10

I pulled into an empty parking spot just across the street from the Capitol Hill Mission. God must have wanted me to do this. Otherwise, a hard-to-get space never would have opened up just as I was adjacent to the shelter. Right?

Mack had eyed me suspiciously all day, as if he thought I were going to don a Hefty bag and take to the streets as Betty. See if I could find out what was going on by pretending to be the infamous bag lady. Not a bad idea, really, except I was more interested in finding her than becoming a target of a crazed killer who might be stalking her.

I'd had Mack bring me back a sandwich when he went out for lunch. I needed to wait around for the security people, and the lunch hour also gave me a chance to do some more detective work on the clothes without being under the scrutiny of Mack the Knife, as I used to call him. Now knives only made me think of poor Van Dyke.

While Mack was gone, I finished going through all the O'Brien and Van Dyke orders, which were set to be delivered to the law firm as soon as the police would let us back in the office. I was particularly interested in the order for Harrison Van Dyke. It was another Giorgio Armani suit, but thanks to our careful inspection system and the fact that we use a lint roller on every garment once it's pressed, there wasn't a single loose hair on it anymore. No blond hairs to tie Van Dyke to Ms. Sexy Voice.

Obviously our driver didn't need to return the suit to the law firm now that Van Dyke was dead. I set it aside. I even toyed with the idea of taking it over to the Van Dyke house myself. I knew it wasn't any Good Samaritan feeling that was motivating me. I wanted to find out what Agnes Burley, the Van Dyke maid, had to say about the murder. But my left brain kept telling me that Mack was right: I should leave that to the police. My only snooping should be confined to finding Betty.

I'd called the Capitol Hill Mission while Mack was still at lunch and asked for Lawrence Baldwin, the director. I'd talked to him and the heads of some other homeless shelters when I set up our clothing drive.

"He won't be in today," a woman's voice informed me.

I asked when the shelter opened for the night.

The woman told me that people off the streets were allowed inside at six-thirty and that the shelter was generally filled to capacity within the hour. "But we have some people who stay here for longer periods of time. They can come and go until eight-thirty, but if they don't call in by then, we give their bed to someone else."

"Could you tell me if a woman named—?"

"Here's your Reuben," Mack said as he came in my office.

I jumped, thanked the person on the other end of the line for her help, and slammed down the phone. I turned to my computer. "Did I tell you we were up twenty percent in volume last month from November of last year?" I asked.

"That's good. . . ." Mack glanced at the blank screen and then back at me.

Officer Valdez appeared just then to pick up the ruined clothes. Two men from the security company arrived a little later, and while they were there, I busied myself out in the plant running the quality-control spot check on my inspectors. I had a list of things I checked when I graded the clothes: Were there any missing buttons, spots not removed from the garments, wrinkles that weren't supposed to be there when the pressers got through, or loose threads or lint on the clothes?

My inspectors were doing a great job. That's why there wasn't anything left as a clue on Harrison Van Dyke's freshly cleaned suit.

"This place is as secure as Fort Knox," one of the men from the burglar-alarm company promised me when they finished.

I doubted that, but it made me feel better all the same. I returned to my office and started calling people to tell them about their damaged clothes. I needed to have them give me estimates of how much each item was worth before I began filling out the claim forms.

It was not a pleasant task, and I kept wishing Mack would leave so I could head for the shelter. I didn't want him to take a notion to follow me.

"Well, I'm taking off now," he said finally as he popped his head around the door.

I finished putting another message on a customer's answering machine, put down the phone, and looked at my watch.

"Is it six o'clock already?" As if I didn't know. "You should have been out of here hours ago."

Mack shrugged. "Call me if there's any more trouble."

"I think everything's okay now."

"So what are you going to do tonight?"

I feigned a yawn, but I have to admit, I was beginning to itch. I could feel another lie coming on. "I'm really beat after last night, so I'm going to crash as soon as I get home."

He nodded his approval. "Well, if you want me to take a run down here this evening and check on the plant, let me know."

"Sure, I'll just give you a whistle. You know, pucker up my lips and blow."

It was a game we played sometimes, quoting famous lines from movies and seeing if the other person could identify them or give the correct dialogue if we had it wrong. But Mack wasn't being diverted tonight.

"Why don't you just try picking up the phone?" he asked.

I waited for a few minutes after he left, just in case he came back or was lurking around outside. I made arrangements for Theresa, my front-counter manager, to close for me. Then I changed out of my dress-up outfit, back into the jeans, sweatshirt, and the purple and green down jacket I'd worn the night before.

As I left, I grabbed a box of clothes for the shelter. We'd already cleaned and given most of the clothes away, but donations were still coming in, so maybe I could make a delivery if I needed to get inside the place.

I carried the box to the van and put it behind the front seat. I felt as conspicuous as if I were wearing a formal gown to a Bronco game. That's what comes of driving the company van when you're going on a stakeout. Maybe I was going to have to reevaluate this whole thing about advertising the business every place I went.

I had lots of time to think about it once I was parked across from the shelter. In fact I was afraid if Betty showed up and saw the van, she might take off, but I wasn't about to park on a side street and freeze my buns off standing in a doorway trying to spot her. Not in twenty-degree weather. Not when the Lord had provided me with my personal parking space.

Thanks to Mack's dawdling around the plant, it was a little after six-thirty by the time I got to the shelter. They'd already started letting people inside. All men, I noticed. So what about the women who needed a place to sleep?

I finally saw a couple of women go up to another door, show something to a man stationed there, and go inside. Several other women showed up later. Betty wasn't one of them, or if she was, she wasn't wearing her Hefty bag.

I rolled down the window to get a better look. Nope, she wasn't around. I shut the window and watched the women disappear into the building.

The homeless shelter is on Colfax Avenue, only a few blocks from my apartment. Colfax runs all the way from one end of Denver to the other. I'd heard once that it was the longest continuous street in any city in the country, but like other facts Nat and I had learned in junior high, I wasn't sure if it was true any longer.

The street had definitely gone downhill since the days when state legislators stayed at a hotel just down the street. Only a short distance beyond was the Colorado State Capitol Building with its gold dome, which had been polished up some years back in a renovation project. Unfortunately nothing could be done for the tarnished image of the street.

The shelter was a freestanding building near a porno bookstore and a fast-food restaurant. The mix of businesses reflects the schizophrenic character of the neighborhood where the homeless and the runaways mix with the young working-class people who live in the Victorian houses and apartment buildings nearby.

The window on the van steamed up from my breath on the cold glass. I took a tissue and cleared it away for about the tenth time. At least it wasn't snowing tonight, which would have obscured my vision completely.

Stragglers kept coming up to the shelter and being admitted during the next half hour. Sadly most of them were alone. Didn't any of them believe in the buddy system?

I fidgeted, trying to find a way to get comfortable in the driver's seat of the van. When I read private-eye novels, the stakeout didn't seem so bad. Maybe it was because the PI was invariably successful in finding the person she was looking for.

When I finally saw one man go up to the door of the shelter and be turned away, I decided all the spaces must be filled. I hoped the guy found another place to spend the night.

But damn it, where was Betty? I'd been so sure she'd show up here. I waited awhile longer in case she was a late arrival, but maybe she'd gone in before I arrived. Now was the time to put Plan C into operation. The Christmas clothes.

I climbed out of the van, grabbed the box of clothing from the back, and locked up before I crossed the street. I knocked on the door of the shelter, and the guard who'd admitted the women shook his head at me.

I pointed to the box.

Finally he unlocked the door. "Sorry, we're full up tonight."

And to think my pal, Nat, said I dressed too fancy ever since I took over the cleaners.

"No, you don't understand. I don't want a place to sleep. I'm from Dyer's Cleaners, and I've brought you some clothes from our Christmas clothing drive."

"Thanks." The man took the clothes, but I could tell he thought that concluded our conversation.

"Also I'm looking for a woman named Betty. She wears a Hefty bag."

"You can check at the desk." He motioned to a woman behind a counter. The place looked like the lobby of a small hotel.

I went over and repeated my description of Betty. "I think she comes here sometimes, and I wondered if she's here tonight. I need to talk to her. It's very important."

"I'll have to check in the dormitory." The woman, who was wearing a volunteer's badge, disappeared through a door to the right. I could see some women inside watching television. They didn't look any different from me, and I couldn't help thinking how any of us could get in that position, given a run of bad luck.

The volunteer came back to the counter. "Sorry, she's not here." I wondered if the woman actually would tell me if Betty was inside and didn't want to see me.

I fumbled in my purse for one of my business cards and gave it to her. "If she shows up, would you give her this card and tell her to call me?"

The woman nodded and tucked the card in a drawer.

I went back to the guard at the door and handed him a card too. "Betty, the woman I just asked about, may be in danger. If you see her around here, would you give me a call?"

He glanced at the card. "I saw her outside last night talking to a friend of hers, but the police showed up about that time looking for her and she took off."

Damn. Why hadn't Stan Foster told me that? No wonder she hadn't come back tonight.

"Well, thanks for your help." I put my hand on the door to push it open, but it was locked. I stepped aside, and the guard opened it for me.

"You know, it's funny," he said. "There was someone else asking about her earlier tonight."

"Someone else?"

"Yeah, a man."

Was the killer that close on her trail? "What did he look like?"

"He's sleeping back there." The guard motioned down a hallway to our left. "That's where we let the transients stay at night."

"You mean the guy is one of the regulars?" I relaxed a little. Maybe Betty had a buddy after all, and I could talk to him. "Do you suppose I could ask him a few questions?"

"I don't know." The guard shook his head doubtfully. "And come to think of it, I never saw the man before today. He wanted to know if anyone around here knew her, and I told him that this guy, Mozart, had been talking to her last night."

My whole body froze. "So is—uh, Mozart here tonight?"

"Yeah, I saw the two guys talking to each other in line and then they both came in here and sacked out."

I wasn't feeling good about this, but I had to ask. "Could

you take me back there and show me the guy who asked about her?"

"I'm not sure."

"Look." I glanced at the tag above his badge, which said his name was Louie. "Look, Louie, I know your director, Mr. Baldwin, isn't here today, but if you'd call him, I'm sure he'd say it was all right." The injection of the director's name seemed to help.

"Mr. Baldwin's out of town, but I'll phone our on-call supervisor about it. You stay here." He locked the front door again and disappeared into an office.

I wondered if maybe I should have him call Foster, but what if the guy took off before the police arrived? I was still debating that option when the guard returned.

"Come on. Follow me."

We went down the hallway and into a huge room with men in sleeping bags and on blanket-covered mattresses on the floor. There was hardly room to walk between them.

Louie had a flashlight, which he held close to the floor so we could thread our way through the mattresses and sleeping bags.

"Will you shut off that damn light," someone growled. Other men yanked the blankets over their faces and scooted down in their sleeping bags as we passed.

I must have been out of my mind to have this poor, unsuspecting guard lead me through the sea of bodies so I could take a look at the face of a man who might be the killer.

But Louie was probably used to breaking up fights and handling surly transients, I told myself. Unfortunately he didn't look that big and strong to me, and suddenly I lost my nerve. I should have had him call Foster and waited for reinforcements. I tried to tug at the back of Louie's shirt, but it was too late.

He stopped at one of the mattresses and said, "That's him."

Like the other transients, the man on the floor had a blanket pulled over his face. All I could see was a dark forehead under a black knit cap. As we looked down at him, he pulled back the blanket and opened one eye. I pulled back from him in fear, but fear gave way to astonishment.

"Oh, shit," I said. "Mack, what are you doing here?"

Mack pulled the blanket away from his face. "What are *you* doing here?"

"I was looking for Betty."

"So was I." He rose to a sitting position. "I was afraid all day that you'd figure out what I was planning to do."

"You never could resist playing a part, could you?" I wanted to laugh, but I was afraid I'd wake up some of the other people.

Mack laughed instead, but at least he didn't give one of his stage laughs that would have awakened the whole room. "You got that right, Mandy."

Someone stirred in a sleeping bag next to him.

"Is that Mozart?" I asked, looking back at Louie. "I'd like to talk to him."

Louie shook his head. "Some of these people get real mad when you wake them up."

"I already talked to him," Mack said. "He doesn't know where she is."

"Will you people shut up," someone yelled.

"Maybe you should hold your conversation somewhere else?" Louie whispered. It seemed like a reasonable request.

"Okay, let's get out of here, Mack," I said.

He nodded and threw his blanket aside. He was still in the navy pea coat he'd been wearing that morning, but he was in his stocking feet. He grabbed his shoes and galoshes, and we followed Louie out to the lobby.

To his credit, the guard didn't get mad about our little mix-up, and when he let us out, he promised to call me if he saw Betty.

"The van's over there." I pointed to the other side of the street, shaking my head. "You really do like to put on an act, don't you?"

"What you talking about?" He grinned and gave me his best imitation of Marlon Brando. " 'I coulda been a contender. I coulda had class and been somebody. Real class. Instead of a bum, let's face it, which is what I am.' "

I wasn't even going to bother to identify what movie the speech was from, not after he dropped the ball earlier in the day on my Lauren Bacall imitation.

When we crossed the street, I noticed a man huddled in the doorway of a building behind the van. It was the guy who'd been turned away from the shelter earlier.

"Hey, mister," I yelled at him. "Go knock on the door again. They have a place for you now."

He didn't respond, but Mack went over and shook him awake. Mack may not be a real boxer, but ever since he played the black heavyweight in a local production of *The Great White Hope*, he thought he was tougher than he really was. Fortunately the man in the doorway scurried across the street to the shelter instead of coming at him with a broken wine bottle.

"Want to go get something to eat?" I asked.

"Sure, if you'll bring me back to my truck."

"What about going down to Tico Taco's?" It was the

Mexican restaurant behind the plant. "I'd like to check and make sure Theresa got the place closed up okay."

Mack agreed, and I got in the van and reached across to unlock the passenger's door.

I started the van and pulled out in traffic. "So what did Mozart have to say?"

"That the cops came around looking for Betty last night."

I nodded. "That's what the guard said, and they scared her away."

"But I bet he didn't tell you *this*."

"What?" I wheeled the van onto a one-way street going south.

"Mozart said Betty was scared because someone was following her. When she took off last night, she said she was going to find a person who might be able to help her."

My hand jerked on the steering wheel, and I skidded on the snow-covered street.

"Who? Did he say what the person's name was?"

"Yeah, he said it was Princess Di."

I pulled the car to a stop at the curb. "You're kidding."

Could Betty have been the person near the fire escape the night before or maybe even the heavy breather on the answering machine? And what if she'd tried to find me after I took off for the cleaners in the middle of the night?

"Maybe we'd better stop by my apartment to see if she's there tonight." I didn't add my worst fear—that we'd find her body in the alley.

CHAPTER 11

McKenzie and I checked the stairwell that led up to my third-floor apartment. Since Nat had told me that he'd waited for me there last night, maybe he'd scared the bag lady away.

As I unlocked the door, I heard a noise inside.

"Watch out," Mack said, trying to push past me.

I flipped on the light switch and caught Spot in the act of jumping off the kitchen counter, where he knew he wasn't supposed to be. He'd overturned a box of Cheerios in his haste to get down, but at least he had the good grace to seem embarrassed about it. Normally he just did what he wanted to do.

I gave him some more dry food and fresh water and checked my answering machine. There were three calls. While Mack checked out the rest of the apartment, I hit the replay button and listened to the messages.

One was from someone at a TV station, who was calling about the bloody suit I'd found. Forget that. The second call was from David. Either he wanted to finish firming up the date for the Christmas party or he was calling to tell me his company wouldn't pay the claim. He left his home number and asked if I'd return his call when I got home. Finally, Nat had called, and he was pissed.

"Some friend you are, Mandy. The cops told me a bag lady gave you the suit yesterday. They even gave me a sketch you made of the woman to run in tomorrow's paper, but the TV stations have already picked it up. You can consider our friendship over. Fini, kaput, zilch, nada. . . ."

I wasn't sure if all his words fit the situation, but I got the point. Boy, I was going to have some fence-mending to do.

"It's not so much the fact that I didn't get a scoop as it is that you lied to me," Nat continued on the recording. "That's what hurts. My best friend, and you lied to me." He hung up.

I felt terrible, and I was itching all over by the time the machine shut off. Foster hadn't told me he was going to release the sketch to the press; I'd thought he'd use it to hand out to the other cops.

"Don't let Nat kid you, Mandy," Mack said. "It was the scoop that bothered him."

"I suppose, but I'd better let him cool off for a while."

Mack and I went outside and looked around the building. I was afraid to go in the alley where I'd seen the shadow of the person last night, and I was glad Mack was with me. It wasn't so much that I wanted a protector as it was that I needed a friend in case we found Betty's body.

Luckily there was nothing there. I had to get over this weird fixation about finding her dead. I wasn't her keeper, after all, but by telling her friend she was going to go looking for me, it seemed to make my responsibility greater than ever. Still, if she'd been so anxious to find me, why hadn't she shown up at the plant this morning?

When I'd convinced myself she wasn't around, I took Mack to dinner at Tico Taco's. My treat. We drove down to Cherry Creek and circled the cleaners first. I checked the back door to see that it was secure. Everything seemed to be okay.

Tico Taco's is in the strip center behind the plant, and Mack and I both know the owner, Manuel Ramirez.

He came up to us as soon as we entered. "I been keeping a eye on your place, Mandy," he said. "I hear about the break-in attempt las' night from Mack, but everythin's okay so far."

He seated us at a booth so that I'd have a view out the window to the back door of the plant. We ordered—fajitas for Mack and the enchilada plate for me—and I slumped back in the seat. Fortunately it had a high back so that I could lean my head against it. I hadn't realized how tired I was until now. I wasn't even hungry.

The waitress brought us a complimentary bowl of green chili salsa and chips. I hoped maybe the salsa's extra-spicy taste would awaken my taste buds, if not the rest of me.

I dipped a tortilla chip into the salsa as Manuel escorted another couple to a booth right in front of us. I ducked my head in hopes they wouldn't recognize me.

It was Eric Jenkins and Ms. Sexy Voice, and suddenly I was wide awake. Now, this could be interesting. Somehow a wisecracking bantam rooster on steroids just didn't seem the type for an attractive receptionist like Pamela Leyton. She'd seemed more attracted to tall, handsome men like Detective Foster.

"Could we change sides of the booth?" I whispered to Mack.

He pulled off his black knit cap and scratched the top of his head as if he were trying to make up his mind. His wiry iron-gray hair always reminded me of a Brillo soap pad.

"Sure, I have to go to the head, anyway," he said finally.

He got up and left as the waitress approached the O'Brien and Van Dyke table. I used her as a human shield as I squeezed out of the booth and slipped around to the other side. Once there, the high back on the booth protected me from view.

I could hear Eric giving the waitress their orders for margaritas. Then his voice lowered to a hum. Damn. I wondered if a water glass to the back of the booth would help. Wasn't that supposed to permit you to hear through closed doors?

I moved out to the edge of the seat.

"Did you ever hear what the argument was about?" Sexy Voice asked.

I leaned out of the booth as far as I dared without revealing myself or risking decapitation by a passing waitress.

"Apparently Harrison was planning to leave his wife," Eric said, "and Frank and little Vancie were all upset about it."

So that must be the fight Nat said Van Dyke got into Friday night. No wonder his father-in-law, not to mention his son, had been angry at him. Already I'd learned something that might get me back in Nat's good graces.

Mack returned to the booth, and I straightened up, but still with an outward tilt to my head as if I had a kink in my neck.

I took one of the napkins and wrote "They're from the law firm where Van Dyke was killed." I made an arrow toward the other booth.

Mack read the note and then made a move as if to put the message in his mouth and swallow it. He settled for sticking it in his pocket.

The waitress brought our food and two margaritas for the next table.

I couldn't hear any more from Eric and Pamela for a while, what with the rattling of dishes and slurping of drinks.

"Do you think it was Margaret?" Pamela asked. "She's not even attractive." The receptionist's voice rose above its seductive level into the range of shrew.

"But she always had a certain vulnerability about her, and that can be quite appealing to a man," Eric said. "Besides, she's had a rough time of it these last few years, what with that jealous ex-husband of hers."

"She's a cow."

There was such venom in her words that I wondered if Pamela was capable of hiring a hit man to kill Van Dyke. After all, those long blond hairs on his jackets did match the length and color of her dye job. What if he'd refused to leave his wife for her, then decided to do it for another woman? I'd have to give that more thought.

Right then some canned mariachi music blasted over the loudspeaker system. Well, forget any chance of conversation at our table, much less the next one. There wouldn't be any more eavesdropping tonight.

It wasn't long before Eric and Pamela left anyway. They'd apparently just come in for a drink. Mack and I ate our dinners, and I drove him back to his car.

On the way I asked him a question that had been bothering me all evening. "If you planned to spend the night at the homeless shelter, why'd you keep telling me to call you if I needed anything tonight?"

He gave me a big smile. "Oh, that was just a diversion. I didn't want you to figure out what I was planning to do.

Same as you telling me you were going to go straight home to bed."

My nose began to itch. Me and Pinocchio.

"Besides, I figured you wouldn't call anyway if I told you to," Mack said. "Don't forget, I've known you since you were knee-high to a pants press."

We'd reached his pickup on a side street near the shelter. "Are you implying that I have a problem with authority?"

"Damn right." Mack winked at me as he started to get out of the van. "Seriously, I been thinking about it, and I could go stay at the plant tonight if you're feeling nervous about it."

"Haven't you had enough excitement for one day, Mack? Besides, now that the story's out about how the police have the suit, I don't think anyone will be coming back to the plant."

"Okay, but if you need anything, just whistle. By the way, the line is 'You know how to whistle, don't you, Steve? Just put your lips together and blow.' Lauren Bacall to Humphrey Bogart in *To Have and Have Not*."

Oh, sure, now he was going to play movie trivia. He'd ignored my effort earlier in the day when I'd been trying to deflect his suspicions from what I was planning to do. Obviously he hadn't bitten because he'd been too preoccupied with his own plans for a kamikaze attack on the shelter.

"Get out of here, will you, Mack? I'm getting cold."

He climbed out of the van and started to close the door.

"And by the way," I said, "that thing about being a bum, it's Marlon Brando in *On the Waterfront*."

I waited until he climbed into his pickup before I drove the few blocks back to my apartment.

Still no sign of Betty, and Spot didn't even bother to come out from wherever he was hiding. No more calls on the answering machine either. Oh, yeah, David Withers had wanted me to call.

It wasn't ten yet, so he should still be awake. I dialed the number he'd given me.

"This is Mandy," I said when he picked up. "Sorry it took so long to return your call. I was out delivering some of the used clothes from our Christmas donation box." Now, why did I have to say that?

"No problem," David said. "I wanted to see if maybe we could have breakfast together tomorrow. I need you to sign the claim forms, and we can talk about the party at the same time."

"Sure, why not?" After all, now that Nat was mad at me, I could always use another friend.

He suggested we meet at eight o'clock for breakfast at Eggs-actly Right, a too-cute breakfast-lunch place that was close to both our places of business. I asked if we could meet at nine in case Betty showed up at the cleaners.

"I heard about her on the news tonight," David said. "It said the suit she brought in may be involved in that murder case over at the Landmark Building. Have the police found her yet?"

"Not that I know of." I glanced at my watch. "But I want to catch the late news and see what they have to say about it. We can talk about it tomorrow."

After we hung up, I took a quick shower, washed my hair, and tried to avoid looking at myself naked in the mirror. A person always knows she can use a little toning up when she looks better in clothes than she does without.

David had told me yesterday morning that he'd begun working out at a gym. I'd have to ask him where he exercised.

By the time I got to bed, the news was on. I caught the

part about the Van Dyke murder, but barely. A local anchorman said the bloody suit had been turned over to the police by me, and showed my sketch of Betty, who was identified as the person who'd found the suit. He said the police were looking for her for questioning as a possible witness, then switched to a reporter in the field. The reporter was shown interviewing Detective Foster, who said some of the blood on the suit matched Van Dyke's blood type. "Told you so, Foster," I said to his TV image.

That's the last thing I remembered until my alarm went off at five the next morning. Time to get up and get to the plant to fire up the boiler for another day of work. After I'd overslept yesterday, I couldn't let Mack down. But was this any way to live? I'd be glad when Mack's turn came next week.

I struggled out of bed and put on a pot of coffee. Spot had come out of his hiding place and was staring at me, so I gave him some more food.

In the bathroom I had another confrontation with my reflection. Mirror, mirror, on the wall, who's the fairest . . .? You should take better care of yourself, Mandy, and start getting more sleep, it seemed to say. Not to mention that you should avoid blows to the stomach. I checked the bruise on my midsection; it was still black and blue, but not as sore as yesterday.

I'd gone to bed with my hair plastered to my head, and now it looked like a flattop worn by deranged paramilitary types. I did the best I could at making repairs before I got dressed.

I put on a red skirt and white blouse that came complete with a black and red Mickey Mouse tie just like the men wore. Since most of my counter employees are women, I wore the tie sometimes just to show what a good job we do cleaning ties. We even have special Dyer's Cleaners pack-aging for our ties in long, narrow boxes.

It took me a while to get the knot right. Wouldn't do to have it all askew when I greeted my customers, and I wondered why men put up with wearing such things every day. The same reason women put up with panty hose, I suppose.

I squeezed into my hose and slipped on my black blazer. By then the coffee was done, and I had a restorative cup with a piece of toast. Just to hold me off until my breakfast date with David.

All that was left was to put on my boots, grab my down-filled jacket, and be on my way. Never mind that my purple and green jacket clashed with the red skirt. I wasn't plan-ning any more trips to law firms, and I figured the customers rarely saw me outside the plant, only behind the counter.

"Bye, Spot," I said.

I swear he looked glad to see me leave.

As I went down the stairs, I wondered about the plant. I was sure the analysis I'd given McKenzie was correct. The burglar wouldn't come around again once he realized the bloody suit wasn't at the cleaners.

It was cold, maybe ten degrees, but the road crews were already sanding the roads, and I made it to the plant by six. It was still pitch-black when I rounded the corner, leading to the back door where I parked. All the stores in the strip center behind the plant were closed. Tico Taco's wouldn't open until eleven, or I'd have suggested to David that we meet there for breakfast.

As soon as I turned into the parking lot, my heart stopped in midbeat. I expelled my breath in a puff that looked like steam from one of our presses.

Double damn. I'd been wrong about someone breaking into the plant again. A dark figure was near the door, and he had what looked like a big plastic bag of clothes in his arms.

I wheeled the van toward the figure. The headlights shone on the person as he grappled with the bag of stolen clothes. He was wearing the same dark ski mask. I stepped on the accelerator. He wouldn't get away from me this time. Not when I was in the van and he was on foot.

He dropped the bag, and I jammed on the brakes so I wouldn't run over the clothes. He took off running.

I turned the wheel and hit the accelerator, but my tires spun in the snow. I willed the van to move; I couldn't lose the guy again. The van spurted forward, but I noticed the pile of discarded clothes out of the corner of my eye.

It moved, and I skidded to a stop. As I slid open the door, I heard a groan. Oh, God, it couldn't be. I heard the sound again and gave up the chase. The man disappeared around the corner of the building as I raced to the bag he'd dropped in the snow near our door. I knew what it was even before I got there. Not what it was, who it was.

It was Betty, and she was crumpled up in a fetal position. There was blood all over, just the way it had been on the suit. It ran down the slippery surface of the Hefty bag like water and soaked into the snow. I was terrified that I wouldn't be able to get help for her before she bled to death.

CHAPTER 12

"Betty, it's me, Mandy," I said, leaning down to her. "Can you hear me?"

She groaned.

"Just hold on, okay? I'm going to get help, but I'll be right back."

My keys were already in my hand. I'd grabbed them when I jumped out of the van. I scrambled to my feet and managed to unlock the door and shut off the alarm even though my hands were shaking. I found one of the sleeping bags that Nat and I had used the other night, took it outside, and covered Betty with it.

"I'll be back in a minute."

As soon as I reached my office, I dialed 911 and told the dispatcher about Betty.

This time it was a man who answered the call. "Don't move her," he ordered.

"I won't. Just hurry."

"Is the person who stabbed her still around?"

"No, he ran away when I arrived."

The man said it was all right if I returned to Betty.

I started to hang up, then stopped. "Notify Detective Stan Foster. He's been looking for the woman."

The man said he would put in a call to Foster.

Betty hadn't moved when I reached her. "You're going to be okay," I said, dropping down beside her and cushioning her head in my lap. "They're sending an ambulance."

"Princess, is that you?" She raised her hand, all covered with blood, and touched me.

"Yes, it's me."

"Somebody stabbed me," she whispered.

"Who was it, Betty?"

"I don't know." She dropped her hand and closed her eyes.

"What about the man who threw away the suit? What did he look like?"

She didn't answer, and I wasn't sure if she'd passed out or died or just didn't want to talk about it. Oh, please, don't let her die.

I don't know how long I knelt beside her, but I kept seeing her attacker in every shadow, afraid he might return to finish the job. Finally an ambulance turned into the lot. There was a police car right behind it. I waved at them from down on the ground.

"She's over here," I yelled. "Hurry."

I got up when the paramedics reached us. They took over and put her on a gurney. It seemed to take forever.

After I told a cop what I'd seen, I asked a medic if I could accompany her to the hospital. "I'm her niece," I said, figuring I needed to be related. The lie didn't even make me itch, but it didn't convince him either.

He said I should meet them at Denver General Hospital. I went to the van, grabbed my purse, and pulled out a piece of paper. I'd just started to write Mack a note when he showed up. God bless him.

"What the hell happened?" he asked, jumping out of his pickup.

"Someone tried to kill Betty. Can you open up for me?"

"Sure, but what about you? Are you all right?"

"I'm fine, but I need to go to the hospital with her." I didn't want to get into an involved explanation about what happened. "I don't know when I'll be back."

Foster still hadn't shown up when I took off in pursuit of the ambulance. I couldn't keep up with it, not without risking a speeding ticket on Speer Boulevard, which cuts through Denver on the bias. By the time I parked at the hospital just off Eighth Avenue and found the emergency entrance, Betty had apparently already been taken to the ER.

A guard stopped me and searched my purse for weapons. I guess that's not surprising since Denver General is where all the victims of violent crimes in the city are taken. In fact a fight had erupted at the hospital recently when two rival gangs, visiting wounded members of their respective groups, met in a hallway on the second floor.

A woman at the check-in desk thought maybe I could provide some information about the victim. Luckily I hadn't told her I was the niece, or she'd have caught on that we weren't related when I didn't know Betty's last name. She told me to have a seat there in the waiting room.

"Will they tell me when they know anything about her?" I asked.

The woman nodded. As I sat down in one of the chairs, I noticed for the first time that I had blood all over my jacket. I yanked it off, folded it so the blood wouldn't show, and put it on the seat next to me.

No one saw my little act of revulsion. At seven in the morning there wasn't much going on in the waiting room. One man was sitting across from me, snoring softly. Apparently he was waiting for someone too.

I sat down and tried to figure out what had just happened. As far as I could tell, this proved that Betty had seen the guy who threw the suit away, and he knew it. Why else would he be waiting for her at the plant this morning? I probably should have kept trying to see if she could give me a description of the guy who'd discarded the suit. Now it might be too late.

I pulled out a small sketch pad from my purse. I always did my best thinking when I had paper in front of me. I didn't write down a list of suspects, though. I doodled. I drew a picture of the man I'd seen running from the door. He'd had on a ski mask. Was there anything about him that might identify him? A limp? His size? What he'd been wearing? I started another sketch.

A cleaner should be aware of clothes, but all I'd really noticed was the ski mask. Maybe a dark jacket and lighter pants. He'd seemed to be about the right height and width to wear the suit. Not a big man, a little on the hefty side, just like Monday night's burglar. I wondered if I'd have been able to catch him if I hadn't seen Betty move, heard her groan. I should have run him down while I had the chance, but with my luck they'd have nailed me for vehicular homicide.

Someone had come up and was standing in front of me. I jumped when the shadow fell across my chair. It flashed through my mind that it was a doctor, come to tell me that Betty hadn't made it, there hadn't been time to do surgery on her.

When I looked up, I saw Foster. He towered above me, usurping my space, but I was glad to see him.

"The woman at the desk said it would be a while before they'll know anything," he said. "I haven't had breakfast. Want to go to the cafeteria?"

"I guess so." I wished he'd get out of my face, though. I stood up, forcing him to move aside. My eyes came about to the level of the breast pocket on his rumpled sports jacket. This early in the morning, and he was already rumpled.

"Did Betty say anything to you?"

"No, I'm sorry."

"I was afraid of that."

I put the sketch pad back in my purse and realized I was rumpled too. I tucked my blouse into the waistband of my skirt and smoothed down the front of my blazer. I had to run to catch up with Foster, who seemed to know the way to the cafeteria. Obviously he'd been here before, and he was holding an elevator for me when I caught up with him.

We went to the basement and down a hallway to the cafeteria. Hanging down from the ceiling was a sign that said GOOD DAY CAFE. Oh, please. I half expected to see "smiley faces" plastered all over. It sure didn't seem like a good day to me, but maybe the name was supposed to give people a positive attitude.

When we went through the food line, I picked up a chocolate-covered doughnut—Betty's favorite—along with a cup of coffee. Kind of a talisman for her recovery. Foster ordered scrambled eggs and some greasy-looking sausages. I'd already paid for my coffee and doughnut by the time he caught up with me at the cashier's stand.

As soon as we sat down at a table, he pulled out his notebook. "So tell me exactly what happened."

I liked it better now that we were at eye level, but he was still distracting with all those sharp, hard lines.

"I already made a statement," I said.

"I know, but humor me."

I ran through the whole thing again. The man, the ski mask, how I'd started to chase him in the van, then saw the movement from Betty's Hefty bag.

"What were you doing at work so early?"

"Someone always gets there at six-thirty to turn up the boiler."

He lost interest in that line of questioning. "So what happened to the man? Did he escape in a car?"

"I don't know. He ran around the side of the building, just the way he did after the break-in. That's the last I saw of him."

"Hmmm."

"What's that supposed to mean?" It sounded as if he thought the man was a figment of my imagination, like maybe I'd done in Betty myself.

"It doesn't mean anything," he said.

"So do you have any good suspects yet?"

Foster shook his head. "We're looking at clients of the law firm now."

That bothered me. Did everyone who worked there have alibis—at five in the morning? I'd been sure the killer was someone inside the firm. What did all my high-tech sleuthing on the computer matter if it was someone on the outside?

"What about Eric Jenkins?" I asked.

"You know him?"

"He comes into the store occasionally, and he's about the right height to wear the suit."

"I'm sorry, I really can't discuss the investigation."

Oooo-kay. So I wouldn't discuss my scenario about how Ms. Sexy Voice with the long blond hair, just like the hairs on Van Dyke's clothes, could have hired—better yet, seduced—someone like Eric Jenkins to kill Van Dyke. I liked that theory, but without a sample of the blond hair for Foster to whisk away to the lab, he probably wouldn't buy it.

I tried anyway. "I saw Pamela Leyton and Eric together in a restaurant last night. They were talking about the case."

"What were you doing—tailing them?"

"No, I wasn't tailing them. I was having dinner and they came in." I thought it best not to say that it was after my stakeout at the homeless shelter.

Foster seemed deep in thought. "It's sure too bad she didn't tell you something," he said.

It took me a minute to make the jump from Pamela Leyton and Eric Jenkins back to Betty. "Yeah, I know."

Foster pounded some catsup on his eggs and started to eat. So what did we discuss now?

"Your order's ready," I said finally.

His fork, heaped with eggs and part of a sausage, stopped midway to his mouth. "What?"

"Your shirts are ready. We got the ink stains out."

"Oh, I'd forgotten about them." The eggs and sausage tumbled off his fork and down his tie. "Damn." He grabbed a napkin and tried to clean up the mess.

"I'm sorry." I handed him another napkin, but I couldn't resist smiling as I watched him dip the napkin into his water glass and try to remove the grease and catsup stain from his tie. All he did was spread the stain to his shirt. I shook my index finger at him. "Not a good idea."

He glanced up with that little-boy look on his face again. "You're saying I shouldn't use water?"

"No, it'll only set the stain."

"You mean I just have to leave it?"

I shrugged and leaned over toward him. Time for some more helpful hints from Mandy the Dry Cleaner. It also seemed like a good opportunity to find out if Foster was married. "Have your wife put some Shout on the stain tonight when you get home."

"I don't have a—"

I started to congratulate myself for finding out his marital status so quickly. Still, I hated the way I'd done it by insinuating that the woman is responsible for all the clothes maintenance in the home.

"I don't have any—what did you call it?—Shout."

I guess I wasn't the Nancy Drew of dry cleaners after all. I still didn't know if he was married or had a significant other.

"I'll be right back." I went to the cashier and asked if she had any club soda. She pointed me to it, and I paid for it at the register. I grabbed a couple more napkins on my way back to Foster.

"What're you doing?" he asked when I rejoined him.

"I'm going to try to get out the spot." I unscrewed the cap, soaked the napkin with liquid, and leaned over toward him. "Club soda's good for removing stains when you don't have anything else."

I lifted the tie away from his chest and pressed the napkin against it. After several applications, most of the stain had been transferred to the napkin. "There, that looks better. Now let's see about the shirt." I put my fingers between the button and the buttonhole and applied pressure to the stain on the shirt.

"Maybe I'd better do that myself," Foster said.

I looked up at him, and he was grinning at me.

"People are wondering what you're trying to do to me."

He was right. It was just a little too intimate a task for a hospital cafeteria, and for a minute I'd had this urge to reach up and kiss him. I couldn't deal with it.

Perhaps removing stains from clothes while a person's in them could be used as foreplay, just like body painting.

"You probably need to learn how to do it yourself anyway," I said, handing the bottle and the napkins to him.

He dabbed at the stain, but without much success.

I would have liked to change the subject, but I have a one-track mind. "About those stain removers like Shout," I said. "You can get them in the laundry section of the super-market—or does your wife do all the shopping?" Now, why did I say that?

He grinned at me again, but this time it wasn't a little-boy grin. It had definite sensual overtones. "Are you asking about my love life?"

"Yes."

"No."

"No, what?"

"No I don't have a wife or girlfriend. What about you?"

"Divorced."

I like to think we might have gotten around to making a date to meet later socially, but right then the loudspeaker crackled to life. "Detective Foster." It was so hard to hear that it sounded to me like someone said *Defective* Foster. There was nothing defective about him as far as I could see.

"Report to the ER waiting room, please. Detective Foster. Report to ER."

"You can stay here if you want," Foster said as he gave one last swipe of the napkin to the stain on his shirt.

"No way." I smoothed down my own perfectly knotted tie, the one I'd worn this morning as an example of our many cleaning services. "By the way, we clean ties too."

We dropped off the trays on a rack for dirty dishes, went up the elevator, and retraced our steps to the emergency room.

The talk about stains and marital status had been a diversion, but now the fear returned. I dreaded what we were going to find out when we reached ER.

A doctor was waiting when we arrived, and he got right to the point. "She had a cut on her arm that wasn't too deep and a stab wound to the chest, which collapsed a lung and caused some ongoing bleeding. We've put a tube inside the chest cavity to suck out the blood and reexpand the lung."

"So when can I talk to her?" Foster asked.

"Is she going to be okay?" My voice was louder than his.

The doctor looked over at me. "If the bleeding stops, she should be okay. Luckily she was wearing all those clothes, but it's still good someone found her as quickly as they did."

"What if the bleeding doesn't stop?" I asked.

"Then she'll require surgery to find and stop the source of the bleeding."

Foster threw me a look that dared me to say anything else. "Can I talk to her?" he asked.

"She's in our trauma room, and she's getting some pain medicine in her IV, but she should be alert enough to answer your questions." The doctor motioned for Foster to follow him. "Just don't stay too long."

I started to go with them. "You'll have to stay here," Foster ordered.

"Hey, look, doctor," I pleaded. "I'm the one who found her. Can't I see her too?"

"No, you can't," Foster said.

"You can see her later," the doctor said. "She'll be transferred up to a room in a few hours."

I stomped over to a chair and sat down. What other choice did I have if the law and the medical profession were both against me? But darned if I was leaving here without talking to her or at least finding out what she had to say to Foster.

Don't stay too long, the doc had said. It seemed as if Foster was gone forever, but I finally saw him coming through the double doors.

"She won't talk," he said. "Looks as if she's scared to death of me. Just huddles down in the bed and says she wants to see Princess Di—whoever the hell that is. These street people have the damnedest names for each other."

CHAPTER 13

I got up, and much as I hated to admit it, I tapped myself on the chest. "Me. It's me. I'm Princess Di."

He looked at me as if I were about one piece short of being a three-piece suit. That was one of Uncle Chet's pet sayings, just like having a couple of buttons missing.

"It's her nickname for me. Di for Dyer, not Diana."

"Jeez." He started back to the trauma room. "Come on, then. Let's see if she'll talk to you."

I couldn't help getting in a jab. "You mean the police are actually going to let a private citizen assist them?"

"Only when they're related to royalty," he said.

I'd been prepared to rub it in some more, but I started to laugh. Humor's always been a good way to deflect my anger or sarcasm. It might even have helped in my marriage if Larry had ever come back with a smart retort—instead of torts, torts, torts all the time.

When we reached the trauma room, a nurse pulled a curtain aside. Betty, her eyes closed, was hooked up to a couple of IVs and lying small in a bed.

But why wouldn't she look small? She no longer had on her version of the layered look. Not to mention that the Hefty bag and the old tan knit cap were gone. It was the first time I'd seen her without the cap. Instead of a few yellowed tufts of gray hair sticking out from under the cap, the tufts now stuck up all over her head like weeds in an untended garden.

"Hi, Betty," I said. "It's Princess Di." The words kind of stuck in my throat, but I managed to get them out.

She opened her eyes and looked at me, then over at Foster.

"I want him to go away," she said.

He pulled the curtain back and withdrew, but I knew he wouldn't get out of earshot.

Her right hand, dirt still under the fingernails, crept out toward me. I started to take it in mine, but she reached up and grabbed my carefully knotted tie and pulled me toward her. Who'd have thought she'd have been that quick when she had that IV in her arm and was getting pain medication.

"It's him," she whispered.

"What?" I gagged as her hand pulled the tie into a noose around my neck. She was strong, too, for someone who was still in the emergency room.

"He's the guy's been followin' me." Her words were firm, even if they were a little slurred.

"Who?"

"That guy that was just in here."

"Stan Foster?" I sounded as if I'd had anesthesia, but I knew what my hoarseness was from. She was choking me with that stupid tie.

She nodded.

For a minute I thought it was lack of oxygen to the brain that made me misunderstand what she was trying to tell me.

"Detective Foster?" I asked.

"Yeah, him," she said.

Could Foster be connected to this in some way I didn't comprehend? I managed to unclasp her hand from the tie and hold it down on top of the covers. "Where'd you see him before?"

"At the shelter the other night. He come around askin' for me, and I had to make a run for it."

Then it finally made sense. Foster must have been the policeman who'd scared her away from the Capitol Hill Mission the night before last. He'd probably been wearing one of his wrinkled plainclothes outfits, and she hadn't even realized he was a cop. Not that him being a cop would necessarily have kept her from running from him.

I was still holding her hand so she wouldn't go for the jugular again. "Betty, listen, he's a policeman just like he says, and he wants to help you. I told him about the suit you brought to the cleaners, and he was trying to find you at the shelter so he could talk to you. He needs to get a description of the man who threw away the suit."

"Is he the guy who tried to run me down that day?"

"Someone tried to run you down?"

She nodded weakly. "Yeah, and I landed ass over elbows between two parked cars."

"Well, it wasn't Detective Foster." I sure hoped what I was saying was true, but it felt right.

Betty thought about it for so long, I thought she'd dozed off. "I still don' like him."

I patted her hand. "Okay, so tell *me* what happened. Did

you get a look at the man in the car or the guy this morning?"

"No, he had a cap pulled down over his face both times, but it had holes in it so he could see me."

That tallied with the information I'd already given Foster about the ski mask.

"Anything else about him?"

"I can't remember." She turned her head, and I was afraid she'd clam up completely.

I took a deep breath. "This is really important, Betty. Can you describe the man who threw away the suit the other day? What did he look like?"

She shook her head back and forth on the pillow. "I didn't see him. Honest."

"Look, you must have seen him. I think he's the one who keeps trying to hurt you. Just try to think."

She squeezed her eyes shut, and a tear dribbled down one cheek. "No, I swear, Princess, I didn't see nobody." She opened her eyes again and pulled her hand out from under mine to stab at the tear.

I believed her, and it sure shot heck out of my theory about the guy seeing her take the suit out of the trash can and bring it to the cleaners.

Betty sniffed. "He must of thought I saw somethin', even if I didn't. Why else would he keep trying to kill me?"

Why indeed? I clasped her hand again. "Well, you're safe now, Betty."

"You sure?"

"Let me get the policeman back in here. Maybe he can get protection for you while you're here at the hospital."

She didn't say anything, which I took for agreement.

Foster slipped back around the curtain. "I'm sorry I

scared you the other night at the shelter, and I swear I never tried to hurt you. If I'd seen someone try to run you down, I'd have arrested him."

Betty snorted. "Yeah, sure. You bobbies are never 'round when folks need you."

"Excuse me?"

"It's a game we play about the British," I said. "You know, Princess Di, tea and crumpets, bobbies. . . ."

Foster glanced over at me as if my tiara were a little off center. "The nurse said we have to leave now." He looked back at Betty. "I need a description of the man who had the suit. It's important that you tell us what he looked like."

Betty frowned. "Didn't you hear me tell the Princess I didn't see him? You were right outside."

I interrupted. "You can still give her some kind of police protection, can't you?"

Foster gave me a butt-out look.

"The killer doesn't know she didn't see him," I said.

He sighed. "I'll see that she doesn't have any unauthorized visitors."

The nurse pulled back the curtain and glowered at us.

I patted Betty's hand. "I'll be back to see you later."

"You promise?"

"I promise."

"Okay, Princess." As I started to take my hand away, she grabbed at the tie again like a lizard zapping an insect out of the air. "Remember when I started calling you Princess Di?"

I nodded.

"I never thought about it standing for D-I-E."

"Clever," I said, extricating my tie from her grasp.

She laughed weakly and winced in pain. "Get out of here so you won't make me laugh no more."

I was glad she still had her sense of humor, but it wasn't a laughing matter. I didn't think Foster had bought her story that she hadn't seen the man with the suit, and if he didn't believe her, the killer sure wouldn't. He'd be coming after her again as soon as she hit the street. And what was I going to do then—take her on as an unwilling, unwanted roommate? No way. It might be easier to find the killer myself, but darned if I knew how.

CHAPTER 14

"I can't get over it," Foster said. "She actually thought I was the killer."

We were on our way out of the ER, but I'd stopped in the middle of the waiting room. I had to remove my tie before I choked to death.

"I can understand why she believed it—if someone tried to run her down earlier in the day." My voice was squeaky as I worked to get the knot out of the Mickey Mouse noose around my neck.

He turned to see what I was doing. Even his tie looked better than mine, wrinkled and grease-stained though it was. Manufacturers should be forced to put disclaimers on ties that they might be hazardous to your health.

"Yes, but I had a uniformed officer with me when I went to the shelter," Foster said.

"Even more reason for her to run." The whole thing at the shelter reminded me of a case of mistaken identity in a Three Stooges movie. I'd thought Mack might be the killer when he decided to go undercover as a homeless person;

Betty had been afraid Foster was the killer because he'd shown up at the shelter in plainclothes looking for her. I wondered if I'd have been so quick to understand her fear if I hadn't had a similar mix-up myself.

I didn't share my thoughts with the cop. He might not take kindly to Mack and me doing a little amateur detecting.

"It had to be the same person who attacked her both times," I said, finally getting the knot out of the tie and pulling it from around my neck.

"Maybe." Talk about noncommittal.

I started walking again, the tie dangling in one hand and my bloodstained jacket wadded up in the other. "You know, I've been thinking. . . ."

"Always a dangerous thing, coming from an amateur." He had the good grace to smile.

"As I was saying, I was sure Betty saw the killer, and vice versa. Maybe he even followed her to the cleaners in hopes of getting the suit back. And that's why he's been on her trail ever since "

"So what's your point?"

"Well, since she didn't see him, I doubt if he hung around to get a glimpse of her. So . . ." I stopped again at the emergency room door rather than go outside and stand in the cold. "So the killer had to learn about Betty when we were talking about her at O'Brien and Van Dyke."

"You mean when you blurted out about drawing a picture of her by the receptionist's desk?"

"Well, yes, but I don't know that you had to put it quite like that."

"Okay?" Apparently he was waiting for the punch line.

"And if that's the way someone found out about her, it

would mean that—uh—" I stopped. No need to tell Foster how I'd nicknamed the receptionist Ms. Sexy Voice. "It would mean Pamela Leyton overheard me, and even if she didn't have anything to do with the killing, she could have told someone else about it."

"Look, you're forgetting that your sketch was on TV last night with the information that we were looking for her as a possible witness."

"Aha," I said triumphantly, "but the killer didn't know that on Monday when she was almost run down by a car."

"We only have her word for the hit-and-run."

He opened the door for me, anxious to get back to his professional detecting. I just stood there. "But you do believe her, don't you, that she didn't see the person with the suit?"

He ran a hand through his curly blond hair. Now it was as mussed as the rest of him. "I don't know. She obviously doesn't like cops, and she knew I was right outside the curtain. Maybe she has a personal street code about not being a snitch."

"I don't care. I believed her, and if you had seen her face, you'd have believed her too."

"Just be aware that I can't do anything to protect her once she leaves the hospital."

"I know, but once the word gets out that she didn't see anyone, everything should be okay, don't you think?"

He finally shut the door, since I wasn't moving.

"You are going to tell the press that she's not a witness, aren't you?"

I waited for him to answer, but he didn't. I guess it was a standoff. I opened the door myself and went down the steps.

"Don't forget your shirts," I said as I reached the sidewalk.

"Oh, yeah, the *order*. Maybe this afternoon."

Good. That meant I'd get to see him again, and hopefully by then he'd have had a chance to consider and be convinced by my logic that Betty really hadn't seen the guy.

He started to his car, which was parked nearby. I ran after him. "Oh, I just remembered, could you see that the hospital has my name so I can visit Betty? I promised her."

He turned. "Sure, it's the least I can do."

"Thanks." I headed for the distant parking lot where I'd left tne van.

"And thank *you* for your help"—he gave me an impish grin—"Princess Di."

My tie might be ruined and my down jacket unwearable, but I felt as if my imaginary tiara was now squarely centered on my head. It warmed me during my cold, coatless walk to the van. I really had helped Foster. I didn't think Betty would have talked otherwise, and I was sure he'd come around to my way of thinking eventually.

If Betty hadn't wanted to say anything, she'd have told me to butt out. She'd done that plenty of times when I quizzed her about her background.

When I reached the cleaners, I went through the front door into the call office. "How's it going?" I asked my morning counter crew.

"Everything's under control," Julia said, looking more rested than she had the day before. That was a good sign, considering the way she'd been overwhelmed by her kids and Christmas.

Ann Marie, the teenager, gave me a curious look. "David

Withers was in a while ago looking for you. He said you had a date for breakfast and you didn't show up."

Damn. I'd forgotten all about him. Now David and Nat both were probably mad at me, but David ought to understand. I wasn't so sure about Nat, but maybe it was time to give the ace reporter a call. Dangle a "lead" in front of him, and he'd follow me anywhere. I hoped. It was my one best shot at getting back in his favor.

I started to the back of the plant. Lucille, who was putting clothes away on the conveyor, stopped me as soon as I walked through the door into the plant.

"No one has picked up that order for the Van Dykes, and it was supposed to be a rush," she said.

It was one of her pet peeves: people who forget their clothes and leave them to overcrowd our conveyor. Never mind that there had been a death in the family. Under the circumstances. I could understand how Agnes had never come back to get them.

"I'll give their maid a call," I told Lucille. "Just leave the order where it is for now." I started to move on, then stopped. "Incidentally, did you notice any more of those long blond hairs on Mr. Van Dyke's clothes when you went through them Friday?"

After all, she was the one who'd pointed out the blond hairs in the first place and compared them with the short red hairs at the neckline of Mrs. Van Dyke's dresses.

"Can't say that I did, come to think of it," she said.

As I passed the press station, Ingrid, one of my silk pressers, yelled at me. I bet it was Ingrid who'd given the wolf whistle when Foster left the plant the day before. I detoured over to her, but I didn't feel like reprimanding her about it now.

"I have to get off this afternoon to go to the doctor," she said, popping her bubble gum at me as an exclamation point.

"What time?"

"One o'clock."

"Okay, if we aren't caught up by then, I can press for a while." In this business a person has to wear many hats.

"Thanks." She blew another bubble, which almost obscured her long, narrow face.

Ingrid is a tall, brassy blonde who has strong oral needs. She almost resigned when Uncle Chet moved here to the new plant and made it a nonsmoking workplace. His edict had eliminated the problem of getting burns on clothes or the claims that we did. But what about gum? Sometimes I thought about trying to make a case for a gum-free environment too.

I waved at Jose, our pants presser, who didn't speak any English. If I ever had the time, I planned to take a course in Spanish so I could at least communicate with him and Hernando Lopez in our laundry. Meanwhile I had to leave the communications to Mack, who had picked up a pidgin Spanish somewhere and was my liaison to them.

Mack hailed me from the spotting board. "How's Betty? Did she make it?" His words echoed off the walls.

"I hope so." I told him what the doctor had said. "But Detective Foster had me talk to her, Mack, and she swears she didn't see the guy who discarded the suit."

"No kidding." He lowered his voice. "Well, I've got some news for you too. They found her shopping cart behind the Dumpster out in the parking lot."

Oh, yes, the shopping cart. Poor Betty. I could understand

how she had forgotten about it under the circumstances, but she'd have a fit when she remembered. She never went anyplace without the cart.

"I can put it in the storeroom until she gets out of the hospital," I said.

"I already did, but not the stuff inside. The cops took that. I heard them saying they found a knife in one of the paper sacks."

"I didn't see the guy toss a knife in her cart." I tried to picture the scene at the back of the plant that morning, but I couldn't even remember seeing Betty's shopping cart. "Well, maybe he did and I just missed it."

"One can only hope."

The enormity of what Mack was saying hit me. "Oh, God. You don't think it could be the knife that killed Van Dyke?"

"I don't know." Mack shrugged his shoulders dramatically. The gesture said volumes about what conclusion he thought the police might make.

I went to my office and called Nat. Time to do some fence-mending, and while I was at it, alert him to the fact that Betty didn't know anything. Just in case Foster forgot to mention it.

Nat usually started work by hitting the police station about noon. I didn't expect to find him at his desk, but I'd leave a message. A contrite apology. No, better yet, a hot tip.

The phone rang. "Yo, Nat Wilcox here."

"It's me, Mandy," I said when I finally realized he wasn't a recording. "Just because you're mad at me, don't hang up."

"I'm not mad. Hurt, undermined, stabbed in the back, cut to the quick . . ."

"Oh, stop it, Nat." Mainly I wanted him to quit making the analogies having to do with knives. "And I'm really sorry that I misled you. I just thought you'd have a hard time keeping your promise to be off the record if I told you about Betty. I knew it wouldn't bother you if I told you something dull about finding the suit in a donation box."

"It was for my own good, right? Like I can't keep a confidence. I'm really wounded."

"I know, and cut to the quick, et cetera, et cetera, but I want to make it up to you. So will you shut up and listen?"

He calmed down, and I told him about Betty being attacked this morning. He already knew that, which is one of the things wrong with having a police reporter for a best friend. But he didn't know that Betty had told me she never saw the guy who threw away the suit. I described the whole conversation.

"I hope you can write something about that," I said in my most cajoling voice. "The killer obviously thinks she saw him, and I don't think she's going to be safe until the word gets out that she didn't."

"That means the police are back to square one. Their possible eyewitness is a bust."

"Yes, so am I forgiven?"

He wasn't ready to let me off the hook yet. "Anything else?"

I told him about the knife that was in her shopping cart, and he perked up considerably.

"Her attacker must have ditched it after he stabbed her," I said, always the optimist. I knew Nat would find out.

I went on to tell him about the conversation I'd heard

between Eric Jenkins and Ms. Sexy Voice the night before at the restaurant. "They said Van Dyke and his father-in-law had been arguing about Van Dyke asking his wife for a divorce. That must have been the fight you were telling me about."

By that time I had Nat eating out of my hand, or at least being civil to me. "I'll check it out," he said.

"So now am I forgiven?"

"I'm thinking. I'm thinking."

Yeah, he was going to let me off the hook. I could tell.

"But next time just tell me the truth," he said. "Okay? I really do mean it when I agree that something's off the record."

"Good, because I itched all night at the plant."

He laughed. "It serves you right, and come to think of it, I should have suspected something when you bolted upright in the sleeping bag and started scratching. I thought maybe you'd just done a bad job of cleaning the damned thing."

"Call me when you get off work tonight and we'll grab some dinner."

"You buying?"

He was really pushing the outer envelope of my niceness. "All right, I'm buying, but then the debt is paid in full."

"Okay. Ciao."

When I hung up, I wondered about the wisdom of suggesting dinner. Nat works until ten or later, and I'd probably be exhausted by then, but maybe I could take a nap first. Besides, isn't a friendship worth more than a good night's sleep?

I'd no sooner put the receiver down than Ann Marie buzzed me with another call.

"Hi, it's David," the voice said.

I wasn't sure if I was up for another apology. "Look, David, the reason I didn't meet you for breakfast was that Betty, the bag lady who came in the store the other day when you were here, was stabbed this morning right outside the plant."

"Oh, God. I'm sorry."

Good. Someone was apologizing to me. "I found her, and I felt like I should go to the hospital with her."

"I understand. Is she going to be all right?"

"I hope so."

"Well, since we missed breakfast, maybe we could get together for dinner tonight, say seven o'clock? I really need to get your signature on that insurance claim."

I'd have preferred lunch, but I was running so late that I probably wouldn't have any time until night anyway. I said okay. Dinner at seven. Weeks without a date and now two dinners in one night. I wasn't sure I could handle that much popularity.

I went out and helped at the counter until Ingrid left for her doctor's appointment. I took over on the silk press and had worked up a real sweat when Nat called back. I swore that my next business project was going to be to get some fans installed above the pressing stations to pull the steam out of the plant.

"What's up?" I asked, wiping the perspiration off my forehead with the back of my hand when I got to the phone.

"Foster says he's not sure Betty was telling the truth about not seeing the guy. He said they'll be talking to her some more later."

I guess I hadn't convinced him, after all, with my powers

of persuasion. "Doesn't he know she's a real sitting duck as long as the killer thinks she saw him?"

"A decoy is more like it, Mandy. Maybe Foster hopes the killer will make another attempt, and they'll nab him."

"Oh, God." Forget about the perspiration on my forehead. Now I was really steamed. "Why don't we just say 'dead duck' and be done with it."

CHAPTER 15

Who cared if I was attracted to Foster? I was beginning to lose patience with him. If he was going to set up Betty in hopes of catching the killer, I might have to reevaluate my feelings for him.

Okay, maybe he didn't have any other leads. So what? That was no reason to make poor Betty a target.

I'd kept out of the investigation just the way any good dry cleaner should. Leave it to the cops. It wasn't any of my business, and what does a cleaner know about murder anyway? But hadn't I been good at creating a profile of the killer by analyzing the suit? And what about the fact that Ms. Sexy Voice could have heard me talking about Betty at the law firm? If the cops weren't going to follow up on the obvious leads, what was a person to do? Not simply stand around the silk press and fume while Betty's life remained in jeopardy.

I mulled over my options as I worked the counter so that my three afternoon counter people, who'd be here until seven today, could take their lunch breaks. By three-twenty the pressers and the people in the shirt laundry were winding down their work for the day, and Al Polaski, my route driver, was back from running the route to offices in the area. He'd finally been able to get back into O'Brien and Van Dyke to drop off the orders that had been waiting since Monday. The suit I'd set aside for Harrison Van Dyke was the only one left on the rack.

Maybe it was time to move to Plan D—a delivery to the Van Dyke house. I went to my office, shut the door, and slipped out of my fancy but wilted red skirt and white silk blouse. I put on a pair of jeans and a sweatshirt that I used for maintenance work and grabbed a jeans jacket off the sofa. My outfit wasn't as professional-looking as the uniforms I'd bought for our driver with the Dyer's Cleaners logo on the back, but it looked a lot better than going out on a delivery in a dress-up suit.

Ordinarily we don't make home deliveries, although I'd given the plan some thought and hadn't discarded it completely. I wanted to see how the business route went first.

But this was different. I would take the orders over to Agnes Burley, the Van Dykes' maid, and see what she had to say. I could well imagine that the house was in a period of grieving and that Agnes probably hadn't had time to even think of the clothes.

I went up and collected the big order off the conveyor and put it on a rolling rack to take out the back door to the van. I stopped to check Van Dyke's address on our computer and wrote it on the ticket so I wouldn't forget it.

"I'm taking care of the Van Dyke order," I said to Lucille, who had returned to marking and pricing clothes for the start-up of work tomorrow. "You won't have to worry about it anymore."

Lucille would be going home at four and so would the rest of my production crew, including Mack. I didn't really want to wait until after Mack left. Like yesterday, he might decide to linger, but meanwhile I had to run the gauntlet by the dry-cleaning machines, where he was king. I grabbed the single suit for Van Dyke off the delivery rack and tried to get past him without getting involved in conversation. No such luck.

"Where you going?" he asked as I attempted to wheel the rack around him. He sidestepped over and stood in my way. For a big man he was even faster than Betty on pain medication.

"It's a courtesy delivery. Someone needs their clothes and can't get in to pick them up."

Cleaners do that occasionally, and we've even been known to deliver wedding gowns to churches so brides-to-be won't get the gowns wrinkled in transit. So why would Mack be suspicious of this? I guess it was just his nature, and I might as well have worn a delivery uniform, after all, to advertise what I was going to do.

He took a look at one of the tickets. "Van Dyke, huh? You just won't leave it alone, will you?"

"They need one of the suits to bury him in," I said, wrinkling my nose to ward off an itch. "The maid called, but she can't get over to pick it up. She's too busy answering the door because of all the condolence calls."

Boy, I should have been able to do better than that. Why not just say I needed to get the clothes off our conveyor? I rubbed my nose with the back of my hand.

Mack looked at the address I'd written on the ticket.

"Why don't you let me deliver the clothes?"

"No, I'm going to do it."

"But I can drop them off on my way home. I'm just about through here, and I go right by that way."

He was really trying my patience. I yanked the rolling rack away from him. "What we have here, Mack, is a failure to communicate."

"*Cool Hand Luke,* right?" he said, referring to our game about famous movie quotes.

"Who cares?" I said. "I'm going to make the delivery, so don't try to stop me. The maid comes in here all the time, and she's a whole lot more apt to talk to me than she is to you. She doesn't even know you."

Mack grinned. "I'll wait around to see what you find out."

"Sure, sure, sure." Uncle Chet might as well have put a codicil in his will that Mack would look out for me forever.

The Van Dyke house is a mansion just up Speer Boulevard from Cherry Creek Mall and right across the street from the Denver Country Club. The swank homes are hidden behind high fences so they can't be seen from the street, kind of like a heavy-set woman who wears a big coat to hide her conspicuous consumption.

The snow was melting fast, thanks to one of the Chinook winds that had blown in this afternoon and makes Denver's winter weather unpredictable. Except for the pines and firs, the trees were all denuded, their limbs like ugly tentacles reaching out as if pleading with Mother Nature to hurry and cover them once again in their leafy finery. Mother Nature was not unlike a dry cleaner, I thought as I tried to picture the Van Dykes waiting anxiously for my arrival with a change of clothes.

A sign at the front gate of the Van Dyke home said NO

SOLICITORS. This from a lawyer yet. I could almost see all of Van Dyke's solicitor-friends stopping and turning around at the gate.

ALL DELIVERIES SHOULD BE MADE AT THE BACK DOOR, another sign proclaimed. Good, that's just where I wanted to go. I drove the van up the curved driveway and around behind the three-story brick house.

RING BELL IF YOU ARE MAKING A DELIVERY. They really were big on signs. I rang the bell and waited. After the third ring Agnes Burley answered. I'd been afraid it would be someone other than the maid.

Agnes is short and stocky and always has trouble reaching our counter with her load of clothes. Her hair is a bright reddish orange, and today she was wearing a pink maid's uniform that fit her like the casing on a sausage. The color was definitely a bad choice with her hennaed hair.

She peered out, finally recognizing me. "Oh, Miss Dyer. What are you doing here?"

"I knew you'd probably have a hard time getting over to the cleaners for that rush order you brought in Friday," I said, "so I thought I might as well deliver it, seeing that I was in the neighborhood." No need to itch. After all, Dyer's Cleaners is theoretically in the neighborhood.

"Well, ain't you sweet? Things have been crazy around here ever since the mister died."

She opened the screen door and reached for the clothes.

"They're pretty heavy. I don't mind bringing them inside."

She stepped back to let me enter.

"And wasn't that strange, you finding that bloody suit?" she said. "That's been quite the topic of conversation around here. Anything new about it?"

Apparently she hadn't heard about Betty yet, and I didn't want to go into it. "I'm sure the police will notify the family before they tell the rest of us anything."

"Like the family would tell me what was going on." Agnes snorted.

"Where do you want the clothes?" I asked.

"Oh, lordy, where are my manners? Let me take them." As we made the transfer, she continued, "I declare, you're the answer to a maiden's prayers—or a maid's anyway." She chuckled at that. "Mrs. Van has a whole bunch more clothes she's been wantin' me to get cleaned. 'Spose you could take them back for me?"

"I'd be glad to."

"I'll take these up and put them away and get the dirty ones for you."

I thought about offering to help her, but I didn't want to get her in trouble for allowing a stranger to traipse through the house. I said I'd wait in the kitchen.

The room was larger than my whole apartment and as sterile and antiseptic-looking as the trauma room where I'd talked to Betty. No amenities for the hired help. Shiny copper pots hung down from above a work area near the stove and sinks, and there were three steps leading up from the kitchen to the rest of the house, no doubt designed by some fiendish architect to make the work harder for serving meals.

I sat down at a table near the work area and tried to think of pertinent questions to ask Agnes when she came back. It wasn't long before the door swung open, and I thought she'd returned.

"Agnes, I need a cup of coffee for this hangover."

A young man wearing green sweats and a pair of

Reeboks came through the door and down the steps. He had whitish blond hair and a marshmallow look about him. I wondered if it was Vance Van Dyke, the son. He didn't look like the elder Van Dyke, not even a shorter, wider version. I sized him up with my mental tape measure. He could have worn the bloody suit, all right, but it might have been a little tight in the waist. That was okay, though, because the button on the suit jacket had been pulled as if someone had strained to get it around him.

"Where's Agnes?" he asked. "And who are you?" He raised an eyebrow, so blond you could hardly see it, and sized me up, kind of like a drunk checking out the action in a singles bar. I half expected him to ask me for my astrological sign.

I took a shot. "I'm making a dry-cleaning pickup that your *mother* requested."

He didn't deny the relationship, and I like to think that it was the reminder of Mom so close at hand that made him lose interest in me. He went over to a Mr. Coffee maker and poured himself a cup of caffeine, then left the kitchen.

Apparently he hadn't connected me with the dry cleaner who'd found the bloody suit, or else he chose to ignore it.

In a few more minutes Agnes returned with a bundle of clothes so high, I could hardly see her head over the top. "I tell you, Mrs. Van is driving me nuts," she said, dropping the clothes in a pile on the floor by the table. "She tells me she wants all the mister's clothes cleaned so she can get rid of them. Him not even in the ground yet, and she wants them out of the house."

Agnes obviously saw that as an affront to the dead; I saw it as an unexpected opportunity to do some more fabricare forensics. I could hardly wait to get back to the plant and start looking for clues, but I also didn't want to miss the opportunity to talk to her.

I fished around in my jeans jacket for a piece of paper. We didn't even have a ticket book anymore. With our computer system, we always input orders back at the plant. "Do you have some paper so I can give you a receipt?" I asked, playing for time.

"Sure," she said. "Want a cup of coffee while you're doing it?"

"If you'll have one with me."

She poured two cups, handed me a sheet of paper, and plopped into a chair next to me.

"I tell you this whole thing is going to be the death of me," she said. "Folks dropping over at all hours to offer their respects. I haven't had a minute to myself since it happened, and if that's not enough, cook's out sick, so I'm having to fix meals too."

"There was a young man who was just in here. Blond, almost white hair, eyebrows so light they were almost invisible. I assume that was Vance."

"That's him." She cupped a chubby hand around a corner of her mouth as if she didn't want anyone else to overhear her. "The Pillsbury Dough Boy is what I call him."

I tried not to laugh, but I couldn't help myself. "Agnes, you ought to be ashamed of yourself."

"Well, you got to have some fun out of life." She winked at me. " 'Specially when you're around a dysfunctional family like this." She drew out the first syllable like a hiss.

I took a sip of coffee and leaned toward her, giving her our code name for Van Dyke's affairs. "Do you think Mr. Van Dyke was killed because of those *business trips* you were telling me about?"

"I wouldn't be surprised," she said, leaning her elbows on the table. "From what I hear tell, the mister wanted a divorce."

"Really? But according to what I've heard, he always had girlfriends on the side—so why now?"

"Beats me." She put her hand up to the corner of her mouth again and whispered, "Besides, Mrs. Van always had *business meetings* of her own, if you know what I mean?"

I let out a deliberate gasp, knowing it would egg her on.

"I never worked weekends, but I always found extra cocktail glasses—some with lipstick on them and some without—when I came in Monday mornings after Mr. Van had been away."

"Really? Were there cigarette butts too?"

"How'd you know about *them*?"

"Oh, I just figured there might be smokers if she was having parties."

"Parties for two is more like it. There were always a couple of butts in an ashtray by her bed."

I was as tense as when I'd kicked the habit myself. "You mean none of the Van Dykes smoked?" I asked.

"Not cigarettes. Mrs. Van wasn't so bad about it, but the mister made me go outside to have a drag, even when it was ten below. Never mind that Vancie was always lightin' up a joint in his room."

I couldn't help thinking of Eric Jenkins, who only smoked after sex. Very interesting. And there was Vance and his joints. We dry cleaners are not smart enough to tell whether a burn is from a cigarette or a joint.

"Did you notice what brand they were?"

"Can't say I did? They were always smoked clean down."

The door to the kitchen swung open again, and Agnes jumped guiltily.

Sybil Van Dyke stood in the doorway. I recognized her from her newspaper photos. She was small and anorexic-looking with short red hair, almost auburn, sculpted around her face. It was the kind of dye job you get at a very expensive salon.

"Who are you talking to, Agnes?" she asked, looking down at me.

Before Agnes could introduce me as the owner of Dyer's Cleaners, I held up the blank piece of paper. "I'm just writing her a receipt for some clothes you wanted cleaned, ma'am. There's no charge for pickup and delivery, and Agnes asked us if we could get the order for her." Hey, I could lay it on as thick as Mack in the acting department. Well, maybe the "ma'am" was a little overkill, and the itching didn't help, but Sybil didn't seem to notice.

I didn't want her to get suspicious about the owner out making deliveries, but what she did pick up on was the word *cleaners*, and she paled. "Oh, dear, you're not from the place that—" She waved her hand in front of her face, almost as if she were fanning herself, and turned to her maid. "I have three guests, Agnes, and we'll need tea."

"Yes, Mrs. Van Dyke," Agnes said. "I'll be right there."

Sybil left, and Agnes went over to a counter and started assembling china cups on a silver tea service. "Didn't I tell you?" she asked. "Never a minute to myself."

"I'm sorry if I upset her."

"Oh, she's always that way, even before the mister died—kind of fluttery, like a moth with molasses on its wings." It was not a pretty picture as I imagined the moth banging into walls, leaving a sugary residue everywhere it hit.

Agnes put some cookies on a plate and added them to the service. " 'Course her husband *did* just die, after all, so it's worse than usual," she said.

Or maybe Mrs. Van Dyke was upset that the police might trace the bloody suit to this house, I thought unkindly, and was ashamed of myself.

I got up, drinking the rest of the coffee. "I'll be right back. I need to get some bags out of the truck so I can put the clothes in them."

Agnes nodded, and I hurried to the van. When I returned, she had disappeared. I put the clothes in two bags as if I were a member of a crime-lab team, concerned about following the correct procedures. I didn't want to destroy any evidence. I wrote out the receipt for the clothes, but I wouldn't need any reminders to know whose order this was.

By then Agnes had returned and offered to help me get the clothes to the car, but I told her it wasn't necessary. "Finish your coffee, Agnes, and I'll bring the cleaning back as soon as we're done."

"Bless you," she said.

When I drove around by the main entrance, I saw Eric walking up the steps to the front door. He didn't notice me, and I speeded up to get out of the grounds before he did.

He wasn't smoking, but I couldn't help wondering if he'd snuffed out Van Dyke, not for Pamela Leyton but because he was having an affair with Mrs. Van Dyke.

Back at the plant I laid out the clothes carefully and started my inspection. A scientist studying a new virus under a microscope didn't have anything on me. Only thing is that a scientist probably doesn't have to endure a kibitzer.

Mack hovered over me like a saleslady in a high-fashion

dress salon. I finally gave him one of the bags and told him to check out the clothes thread by thread.

"By the way," Mack said, "I bet you don't know who actually said that line in *Cool Hand Luke* about having 'a failure to communicate.' "

"Paul Newman said it," I said. "He *was* Cool Hand Luke."

I knew I was wrong by Mack's gleeful look, and I knew he was going to tell me who said it whether I wanted to know or not.

"Strother Martins said it."

Whoever the hell he was, but Mack knew his films, so I didn't argue with him.

Mack chuckled. "You owe me a dollar."

Sometimes I thought I played entirely too many games with people. Movies with Mack, the British with Betty, and code names for affairs with Agnes.

There was nothing in the pockets of Van Dyke's business suits. No dandruff on the shoulders. A few stray silver hairs on the collars that looked as if they'd belonged to Mr. V.D. himself.

Now I'm getting as bad as Betty with the nicknames, I thought. Maybe it was time I grew up, but I swear I hadn't been thinking of sexually transmitted diseases when I came up with it.

Mack and I worked our way through the clothes. It wasn't until I got to the leisure stuff that I found anything significant. And even then there were no long blond hairs on his ski sweater where Ms. Sexy Voice might have cuddled against him. No blond hairs on his cableknit or the smoking jacket with the velvet lapel. But what I did find was even more interesting.

"I think maybe Van Dyke really did have a new girl-friend," I said triumphantly, picking a shoulder-length dark hair off a blue turtleneck. The hair had the crinkled look of a curly perm.

Together Mack and I found several more, clinging to his sportswear like Velcro. Yep, it looked as if old V.D. had dumped Ms. Sexy Voice just before he died and taken up with some brunette with the wet look.

CHAPTER 16

I put the incriminating hairs on a piece of tissue paper that we use to stuff the sleeves and bodices of dresses before we bag them. Then I opened a drawer at the marking table and pulled out a Ziploc sandwich bag.

The Ziplocs are what we use for items that customers leave in their clothes. Good for a piece of costume jewelry or occasionally the real thing. Maybe even money, small change, pens, receipts. You name it. We always attach the forgotten item to the ticket so it can be returned to the customer when he or she picks up the clothes. Only things we don't return are the stuff like condoms and controlled substances. So sue us.

Carefully I shook open the sandwich bag and placed the dark hairs inside.

"What you going to do with them?" Mack asked.

"Call Detective Foster and give them to him." As far as I was concerned, they were genuine clues to what had been going on with Van Dyke just before he died.

"What mischief you got planned after that?"

I thought of my crowded social schedule. Two dinner engagements in one night, and now I had to squeeze in Foster. "A lot more than I'd like to have planned," I said, wondering how I was going to work in a trip to see Betty. "Are you busy tonight?"

"I have a rehearsal for *Twelve Angry Men*. I'm playing a juror. Don't you remember?"

Hey, I'd been distracted lately, but I tried to cover for it. "Of course I remember. I just didn't know you had a rehearsal tonight."

"So what do you want?" he asked. "A little sleuthing before or after?"

"I wondered if you could go see Betty for me. When I call Foster, I'll ask him to okay your visit."

His whole body seemed to recoil. "I don't think so."

Was he refusing the request because Betty was *just* the resident bag lady? It wasn't like him.

"I'm sorry." He dropped his head sheepishly. "I—I get a little queasy in hospitals."

Here was a man who was unafraid of waking up sleeping transients in doorways and yet he was fearful of hospitals and cops. I love people's idiosyncrasies, and I'd have to file that one away to investigate when I had more time.

He pulled himself up to his full six feet one inch and squared his wide shoulders. "Maybe I could pretend I'm a doctor—like I was researching a part for a play. Yeah, then I ought to be able to handle it."

"I'd really appreciate it, Doc. Just tell Betty to take two aspirin and I'll see her in the morning."

* * *

David arrived at the cleaners at two minutes to seven. Mr. Punctuality. I told him to have a seat in one of the gold velvet chairs near the door while we finished closing out.

Poor guy. He was kind of cute in a teddy bear sort of way, but he really didn't have any clothes sense. He was wearing a neatly pressed charcoal-colored suit, a pale blue shirt, a darker blue tie—and green socks. He must be color blind; that was the only explanation I could think of for why there was always something a little out of kilter about his appearance.

I'd changed to a powder-blue wool suit and a gray silk blouse. We blended very nicely except for the socks.

But wouldn't you know, while I hurried to get ready for dinner date number one, Detective Foster showed up—all tall, blond, and handsome. Talk about bad timing. Not only that. He wasn't rumpled. He had on a freshly pressed shirt and slacks, no tie, and the rumpled clothes were in his arms.

He paused in front of two paintings on the wall opposite from my mural. He wasn't in any hurry.

"Are these your paintings too?"

"Yes," I said as I tossed a bag of dirty clothes into a cart under the counter.

The call office made a perfect place to display my art. The two huge paintings currently on exhibit were of striped fields out east of Denver—some golden with wheat ready to be harvested, some brown and fallow. The jagged outline of the Rockies was in the background. They were all straight lines, like Foster's face.

"They don't look real either," he said, apparently referring to the remarks he'd made earlier about my mural, "but I have to hand it to you. That sketch you drew of Betty really did look like her."

"Thanks." I grabbed the cart filled with bags of dirty clothes and started to wheel it back to Lucille's mark-in table.

He came over to the counter. "Ever thought of giving up your career in dry cleaning and becoming a police sketch artist?" He grinned at me so nicely, I almost forgot he was here on business. "So what's this message I got about you having something for me?"

I looked over at David, who was drumming his finger-nails impatiently against his briefcase, which probably held the complete record of every insurance claim we'd ever filed. I know there'd been a fire in the old plant one time, and Uncle Chet had filed a substantial claim for the ruined equipment and merchandise.

"Will you excuse me, David?" I said, going over to him. "I have some business I have to take care of back in my office."

He nodded pleasantly enough, but I could tell he wasn't happy about it. I was half afraid he'd insist on coming with us.

I flipped the sign in the door to CLOSED and told Sarah and Theresa that they could go on home. "I'll turn off the lights before I leave."

I took the cart of dirty clothes as far as the mark-in table and led Foster on through the plant to my office. Our foot-steps echoed in the empty building, but at least this time there were no curious employees to stop the presses or give out wolf whistles as we passed.

"You were able to put McKenzie River's name on the list to visit Betty, weren't you?" I asked, referring to the mes-sage I'd left on Foster's voice mail earlier in the day.

He said he had, and I was relieved. Mack wouldn't have taken kindly to going to the hospital and being turned away.

I turned on the light in my office and went over to a desk drawer. I pulled out the Ziploc bag and handed it to him.

"What's this?" he asked.

"It's some dark hairs we found on Van Dyke's clothes."

He held the Ziploc up to the light and looked at the hairs. "We can't use these as evidence. To have any merit in court, we have to collect hair or fiber samples ourselves."

"Oh, I didn't mean for them to be used as that kind of evidence."

"What did you mean?"

I explained how the maid had given the clothes to me to be cleaned so that Van Dyke's wife could get rid of them. I emphasized the words *get rid of* so Foster would know we were dealing with a widow who couldn't even wait until her spouse was buried in the ground. I decided not to tell him how I'd gone over to the Van Dyke house unsolicited to get the clothes. Foster probably wouldn't like me being any-where in the vicinity.

"So?" he said.

"So remember how I told you about the blond hairs we used to find on his clothes? Apparently Van Dyke found himself a new girlfriend recently, and this could bring up a whole new line of questioning."

"Like what?"

"Like maybe when he switched girlfriends, the blonde hired someone to kill him—or maybe even Mrs. Van Dyke did. I understand he'd asked for a divorce."

"How do you find out these things?"

My remarks must be on target. Otherwise Foster probably would have called them as "hair-brained" as the packet of evidence I'd just given him.

"Is there some dark-haired beauty with a curly perm in the picture?" I asked.

"You know I can't tell you that."

"Maybe someone"—I paused—"named Margaret?"

"I'm sorry, I can't discuss the case."

Okay, so he was still playing it close to the vest, figuratively speaking. You'd think he'd be grateful for all my cleaning tips and throw a few helpful hints in my direction.

"Well, what about Eric Jenkins?" I asked. "I still think he's connected to all this somehow."

"Damn it, Mandy, will you just drop it?"

"At least you ought to be able to tell me something about Betty," I said. "Have you decided whether you believe her?"

"We're still questioning her."

"What about the knife? One of my employees said you found one in her shopping cart."

"Has it ever occurred to you that Betty might have killed Van Dyke herself?"

I hoped he was just playing devil's advocate, but I couldn't let the question go unchallenged. "Give me a break. You don't really think a bag lady's going to go to the twelfth floor of a high-rise and kill someone. Dressed in a man's suit besides."

"Who can tell what she wears under that plastic bag, and for all we know, she could have used the suit to swab up the office."

"So how'd she get in? It's a security building, isn't it?"

He nodded. "But no guard at night. Just a card and an employee code that you need to get through the entrance."

He surely didn't believe that Betty would use such a sophisticated form of entry to get inside a building. In fact

Nat was probably right. Foster was simply planning to use her as a decoy to flush out the killer.

Foster must have read my mind. "Incidentally what's the idea of telling a *Trib* reporter that Betty didn't know anything? It had to come from you."

I didn't even bother to lie about it. "Look, I'm sure she didn't see the killer, much less *is* the killer, and the only way she's going to be safe is if the real killer knows she can't identify him." I got up so he'd know the discussion was over.

I didn't want to lose my temper completely, and after all, David was waiting for me up front. I started to the front of the plant, where I had a few questions for David. I was hoping he'd be more cooperative than the cop.

Foster rose and followed me. He stopped about halfway there. I'd been waiting to see how long it would take him to remember the bundle of clothes under his arm. Not yet apparently.

"By the way," he said, "I've been thinking about what you mentioned earlier. I don't think we said enough about Betty Monday morning at the receptionist's desk that anyone could have figured out what we were talking about."

"Then why did someone try to run her down at the shelter that night?"

"My point exactly. I think she saw someone, but she's still playing games with us."

Balderdash, as the British would say. I continued walking.

He finally remembered the clothes. "Oh, by the way, I brought you some more cleaning," he said when we reached the front counter, "and I guess I could pick up my shirts now too." He put down the bundle he'd been carrying, along with the Ziploc bag of clues, and started going through his pockets for the ticket.

Never mind that the cleaners was closed and the computer was down. I was beginning to get aggravated with him. We'd have to put his new order into the computer tomorrow, but meanwhile he didn't need a ticket for his shirts.

I told him so and glanced over at David. "It'll be just a minute more."

I went back in the plant, yanked Foster's order off our shirt conveyor, and hung it on a slick rail at the counter when I returned. I ripped the ticket off the poly bag, and when he handed me a twenty-dollar bill, I gave him change out of my purse. I'd reconcile the bill and put the money in the till in the morning.

David had moved up beside Foster while I was gone, ready for our hot date. He'd set his briefcase on the counter, reminding me that it might not be all fun and games. He was probably going to tell me he couldn't okay the claim after all.

Foster started to take the shirts off the rail, then stopped. "Say," he said, "would you like to go out and have something to eat after you finish up here?"

Before I could answer, David jumped in. "I'm afraid she already has a date."

Foster looked over at him and flushed a becoming shade of crimson. "I'm sorry. I didn't realize the two of you . . . ." He motioned between David and me as his voice faded away and he headed for the door. "I'm really sorry."

It was hard to stay angry at a cop who could blush and was absentminded, but at least he'd remembered *my* evidence. He must have stuck it in a pocket while I was gone.

"You forgot your shirts, Detective," I said as I pushed his current order into a dirty-clothes bag. I recognized the tie and rumpled sports jacket he'd been wearing earlier in the day.

"Right, the shirts." He slapped himself on the forehead as he came back to the counter and grabbed them off the rail. He clutched them in his arms in a way that was guaranteed to wrinkle them. Maybe I should suggest he get the shirts folded and boxed next time if he were going to treat them that way, but I wasn't going to do it now.

Before the door closed and locked him out, he stuck his head back inside. "Hey, I'm really sorry."

CHAPTER 17

David suggested we go to a Chinese restaurant in what's called Cherry Creek North, a block over from the mall. That's where Maggie Moorehead, the woman who'd been in the cleaners during Betty's visit, managed a high-priced dress store.

The restaurant was called Charlie Chan's, perhaps a sign that I'd moved into high gear in my role as an investigator.

I'm not that fond of Chinese, but I figured it was light enough fare that I'd be ready for a second meal by ten o'clock when Nat got off work. Besides, I'd never mastered the art of chopsticks, and that should cut down on my intake.

"Smoking or nonsmoking?" our Chinese host asked.

David gave me that uncertain look that people who don't know each other well get when they're confronted with the choice.

Since he seemed indecisive, I said nonsmoking.

Our host seated us at a corner table covered with a white linen tablecloth and proceeded to light an oil-based lamp that gave us all the secondhand smoke we needed. "I hope you don't mind," I said.

"No, I used to smoke, but my ex-wife didn't like it. I was tempted to start in again after she left, but I didn't."

"You're stronger than I am," I said. "I'd just quit smoking when my husband, Larry, told me he'd found someone else. Instead of crying or going into a jealous rage, my first reaction was 'I think I need a cigarette.' "

David laughed.

"I was able to quit eventually only by throwing myself into my art. Particularly clay projects where I pretended I was wringing Larry's neck."

A waitress came over, and David asked me if chicken kung pow and sweet and sour shrimp would be okay. I nodded, and he instructed the waitress to bring us a couple of bowls of rice on the side. He appeared to be a sophisticate when it came to Chinese food; personally I'd have ordered the special because I never could remember what any of it was.

As soon as the waitress left, David got right down to business. He had me sign some papers and then he handed me the claim forms for my customers' clothes. "You'll have to get the value of the clothes from them and give it to me." I already knew that, but I nodded agreeably as he slipped the paperwork I'd signed back in the briefcase and closed it. "That should take care of business."

I couldn't believe he wasn't even going to scold me for not having the burglar alarm hooked up to my office window, but never look a gift horse in the mouth, or as David had said when he tried to make a joke, a clotheshorse.

"Why didn't your uncle put in motion detectors when he

installed the rest of the system?" David asked. " It would pick up any movement in the plant after hours."

"It was because of the cat," I said. "But I moved him to my apartment."

"So maybe you should consider motion detectors now. I'll send someone over to analyze your security needs."

"Good," I said, anxious to get to what was really on my mind. "By the way, do you know much about security systems?"

"A little. Why?"

I leaned to the left so that I could still see David as the waitress arrived with our dinner. "Well, I was just wondering if you know anything about the kind of system where you can get into the building with a card and an access code that opens the lock mechanism."

"Are you talking about office buildings?"

"Yes. Don't you think it's unlikely that someone like Betty, the bag lady, could get in a building that way?"

"You mean the police think she murdered that lawyer?"

"I don't know, but the police are still questioning her. Detective Foster—the man who was just in the cleaners— thinks she's holding back."

"So that's who that guy was. I thought it was just someone hitting on you."

I couldn't help but smile. "No, he was there on business."

I was glad David didn't ask me what kind of business. The hairs in the sandwich bag were a little hard to explain, so before he got around to it, I said, "Anyway I was just curious about how tough it would be to get into a building like that."

"Well, I suppose she could have found a card and the access numbers in a garbage can someplace, just the way the papers said she found the suit. But what would seem more likely is that she could hang around the building, and when someone came out, she could slip in before the door actually closed."

He dished up some of the shrimp and chicken dishes on top of his rice and began to use the chopsticks as if he were an old China hand. I watched in awe at both his dexterity and his explanation of how Betty could have gotten into the building.

Still I couldn't see her riding the elevator up to the top floor, killing Van Dyke, and then mopping up the floor with a suit she found in our delivery closet. It made more sense that someone with his own access card and code number had entered the building and murdered the boss. Someone like Eric, who might have been romancing Mrs. Van. That's what I really wanted to talk to David about.

I placed a small serving of both dishes on my rice and tried to look casual as I successfully skewered a piece of chicken. "Remember when you were at the cleaners Monday morning? I noticed that you were talking to Eric Jenkins outside the building. I wondered if you know him very well?"

David stiffened. "Better than I'd like to."

Good, maybe I was about to get some dirt on Eric.

"Why do you want to know?"

I shrugged. "I just wondered if you knew anything about his personal relationships?"

"All I know about him is"—David gripped one of the chopsticks in both hands—"he represented my wife in our divorce. He's a real bastard."

I mixed my food around in the bowl of rice, afraid I'd

opened up old wounds that I'd been hoping to avoid tonight. "I'm sorry. I didn't realize that's how you knew him."

"He's an ambulance-chasing, skirt-chasing bastard."

I didn't know what to say to ease the pain, so I studiously lifted a shrimp up to my mouth.

"I'm sure he was having an orgy with my wife all the time he was representing her." David squeezed the chopstick so tightly that it snapped in two with a cracking sound.

I jumped, and there went the shrimp. I'd lost my grip on the chopsticks, and the shrimp went flying across the table, hit David's lapel, and disappeared into his lap. And I'd thought Foster was clumsy when he dropped his eggs down his tie.

David didn't seem to notice the airborne shrimp because he was staring down at his broken eating utensil as if it were Eric's broken body.

If Eric was the one who'd been murdered, poor David would have been at the top of my suspect list. As it was, I was reminded of how I'd squeezed the clay together, pretending it was Larry's neck.

"Excuse me, David," I said meekly, "but one of my shrimp got away from me. It may have landed in your lap."

He looked down and picked up the shrimp.

"I'll pay for cleaning your suit if it left a stain," I said.

He dangled the shrimp in the air, and since he didn't seem to know what to do with it, I suggested he put it in my empty teacup. Betty and I just weren't much for drinking tea, despite our British heritage.

Finally David picked up a fork and resumed eating. I stuck stubbornly to my chopsticks as I tried to think of a less volatile topic of conversation.

"I've been thinking that I should start working out," I said. "Where do you go?"

"What?" His mind was obviously still back on the divorce.

"To work out? Remember when you were in the cleaners the other morning? You said you'd just come from the gym."

"Oh, yeah, sure."

"I was thinking maybe I should start doing some exercising myself." I didn't add what I'd planned to say about being in mourning long enough from my own divorce. Not after his explosion.

"Well, it's a Nautilus over on the other side of town," he said. "On Jewell and Wadsworth, near where I live."

"Oh, too bad." I held up another shrimp with my chopsticks, pleased with myself, and popped it in my mouth. "Maybe we could have worked out together if it had been in this neighborhood."

When I ate my way down to the rice, I gave up. How anyone could be expected to pick up tiny kernels of rice with chopsticks was beyond me.

After a period of sulking David finally got around to telling me about the party Friday night. He'd pick me up at six-thirty, he said. I'd have to make sure to leave work early so I'd have time to get home and put on something dressy.

It also meant I'd have to get something dressy. I might have enough clothes to look fashionable at work, but my cocktail wardrobe was woefully lacking. I guess I really had been in mourning since Larry left. All I had was one black all-purpose dress that was a little the worse for wear. Maybe I'd go shopping tomorrow.

David dropped me off at the plant. The cleaning crew that

TAKEN TO THE CLEANERS   177

comes in once a week was inside, but I didn't bother them. I'd already talked to their boss about the burglary, and I needed to hurry home for my second dinner date that night.

Spot met me at the door, wearing an aggrieved look. I fed him and checked my answering machine. Three calls, and as it turned out, none of them good news.

The first was from Foster. "I do have something I need to come clean about," he said in response to my recorded message. "Apparently I forgot to pick up that plastic bag you gave me. Like I said, it's not really that important . . ." Thanks a lot, fella. ". . . But I'll try to stop by tomorrow and get it. I guess when I picked up the shirts, I just forgot about it. . . ."

He wasn't fooling me. He'd been so discombobulated by my having a date that he got rattled. I liked that.

The answering machine beeped for the second message.

"Yo, Mandy," Nat said. "I'm going to have to take a raincheck on our dinner tonight. How about tomorrow?"

Great, and after I'd eaten only what I could pick up with the chopsticks, I was still hungry.

"Incidentally," Nat continued, "the knife they found in Betty's shopping cart wasn't the one that was used to stab her. They're pretty sure it was the one that killed Van Dyke. Betty claims she found it in a trash can down the street from where she found the suit."

Just the thing I'd feared. No wonder Stan Foster had been making those wild accusations about Betty killing the lawyer herself. I hoped the third message would be better news. No such luck.

"Hi, Ms. Dyer, this is the doctor, and I've just finished my rounds." It took me a minute to realize it was Mack, disguising his voice. "I talked to Betty, and she said they think she can get out in a couple of days. They're trying to find a place to send her after that, but she says she's mad as hell and she ain't going to take it anymore. She claims there isn't a nursing home built that's strong enough to hold her."

Swell, Mack is mixing his movie metaphors, and Betty is planning to bust out of Shady Rest.

CHAPTER 18

I searched the plant for Foster's bag of evidence as soon as I arrived at work the next morning. It wasn't there. The cleaning crew had been there the night before and probably threw it away. No matter. I managed to find a few more incriminating hairs and put them in another Ziploc bag for Foster's arrival.

I'd called Nat the night before and chewed him out about standing me up. I told him my suspicions about Eric Jenkins and how Foster was being tight-lipped about it. Nat said he'd check it out.

He called me back at the cleaners just before I left for Denver General at ten-thirty.

"Yo, Mandy, I hate to tell you this, but they say Jenkins has an alibi."

"Really?" I was disappointed. "Who's 'they'?"

"Can't say." He was probably smiling his nearsighted Mona Lisa smile again. "But they're very reliable."

"So what's the alibi?"

"Haven't been able to find that out, but I will."

I thanked Nat, hung up, and detoured by the florist on the way to the hospital to buy Betty a big bouquet of—what else?—daisies. After all, Dyer's was the fresh-as-a-daisy cleaners, and I figured I might as well stay with the theme.

When I walked into her room, I almost didn't recognize her. She looked like a whole new woman, thanks to an obvious application of soap and water. Her hair was no longer that yellowish gray that had been in tufts yesterday in the recovery room. Apparently you really can get the yellow out. Now it had a steel-gray quality to it that fit her flinty personality.

Someone had piled the hair in a topknot on the crown of her head, and she looked like an aging Cockney flower girl in Trafalgar Square. I handed her the daisies to complete the picture.

"I never had no flowers before," she said, giving me her gap-toothed smile. She grabbed the bouquet to her chest with a scrubbed hand, squashing it the way Foster had smashed his freshly pressed shirts the night before.

So much for the niceties. She got right down to the nitty-gritty. "Did you hear what they're tryin' to do to me—send me to an IN-STEE-TU-TION somewhere?" She said it like four distinct and very ugly words. "Well, I ain't a-goin'."

I was wearing a rose-colored suit with a pink shell underneath. No way was I going to wear another tie when I came to see the bag-lady-cum-choker. I'd even rejected wearing the fake pearls I ordinarily wore with the suit, and God forbid, no drop earrings in pierced ears. I wasn't about to give her the opportunity to get hold of any part of my accessories, much less my person.

And I had news for Foster. She wouldn't have had to

bother stabbing Van Dyke; she could have strangled him to death.

"Look, Betty, it wouldn't be so bad going to a nursing home," I said. "Just until you get your strength back."

"No siree. They get you in one of those places and they keep you there. Put you in a straitjacket, and they never let you go."

I didn't bother to point out that a nursing home wasn't a mental hospital. I figured Betty already knew the difference, maybe from personal experience.

"They ain't taking me nowhere, and that's it." She folded her arms, no longer attached to the IV tubes, across the flowers in a gesture of defiance. For the first time I noticed the bandage where she'd been stabbed on her left arm.

"Why don't you let me get a glass or something for the flowers," I said, "before you decapitate them."

She gave them up without a fight and watched as I removed the green paper from around the stems and stuck them in a pitcher full of water. The nursing staff might not like my confiscating the pitcher, but the bouquet wouldn't fit in a glass.

I set the arrangement on a mantel across from the bed and underneath a television set on the wall. That done, I leaned against the mantel, bowed my head, and prayed for sanity to keep me from doing what I knew I was about to do.

"Well, maybe . . ." I didn't look at Betty, just stuck my arms straight out in front of me as if trying to push myself away from a really bad idea. "Maybe—uh—maybe you could come home and stay with me for a few days, just until you're well." It sure sounded like me saying those words, but why was I doing it? I must be out of my mind. Like the hatters of Jolly Olde England who used to go crazy from the glue they used on the hats.

"You'd do that for me, Princess?" Betty asked in wonderment.

Yep, I was crazy, all right. Me and the Mad Hatters. "Sure," I said, turning to Betty with a goofy smile—as if I actually believed it was a jolly good idea. "Not to change the subject, but do you mind telling me where you found that knife that the police think was used to kill Van Dyke?"

"Like I told the cop, I found it in a garbage can just down the street from where I found the suit. I try to get around early Monday mornings right before the trash truck comes because that's when folks throw out the best stuff."

"Are you sure the trash truck was due that morning?"

"Sure as my name's Betty." Her eyes kind of twinkled as she said that, because only she knew what her real name was. "Bout seven-thirty is when they come 'round."

Did that mean the person who'd tossed the stuff worked or lived in the area and knew the trash would be picked up in a few minutes? It was something else to think about if I ever had the time.

"Was the knife just out in the open in the trash can?"

Betty shook her head. "Nope, it was all folded up inside a shirt, and I figured it would be good for peeling apples, so I kept it."

I perked up. "What did you do with the shirt?"

"It was all nasty, so I threw it back in the trash can."

Too bad. For a minute I'd hoped she'd kept it and that it might have laundry markings that would lead Foster to the killer.

"Well," I said, "I guess it makes sense that the guy would dispose of the suit and the knife in separate places, but did you maybe see anyone at that other trash can—the one where you found the knife?"

"No, Princess, I swear I din't see nobody at neither one, but I did remember somethin'." She smiled at me as if proud of herself. "The guy who stabbed me had funny shoes. I saw them when I tried to kick him."

"Funny shoes?" I asked, like a parrot picking up on a favorite sound.

"Yeah, I told that cop already. They had bows on them."

I frowned as I tried to get a mental picture of the shoes. "You mean tassels?"

"Yeah, whatever. You do believe me, don' ya?"

"I believe you." I sighed. "Okay, let me go find someone here at the hospital and see if I can make arrangements for you to come to my place for a few days."

"Thanks, Princess. Old Prince Charlie was a fool to let you go."

"You better believe it, Betty." I was the one who was a fool for bringing a bag lady home to share my studio apartment. Spot and I could hardly get along together in that small a space.

CHAPTER 19

It took me until nearly one o'clock to find a social worker and make arrangements to take custody of Betty the next morning when she was due to be released.

"I'm so relieved," she said. "I hated to turn her out on the streets, and there aren't many places that take people without insurance. I'd been trying to find a homeless shelter that would let her stay there for a few days, but there are so few of them that have accommodations for women."

I asked if I could call Foster from her office to tell him I was going to take Betty home with me.

"You crazy?" he asked.

I'd already convinced myself of that. "Yes," I said, "but until you solve the case, I don't want her out wandering the streets."

"That's admirable of you." I wasn't sure if he meant that as a compliment or not. "But seriously, I'm glad to know where she'll be if we need to talk to her."

"Betty just told me she'd remembered that the guy who attacked her had funny shoes. Does that help you?"

"Oh, sure, funny shoes with bows on them. And curled-up toes like they belong to a court jester, no doubt."

Didn't men know anything about shoes either. "I think she meant tassels."

"Oh." Foster sounded as if he'd have to think that one over for a while. "You got my message last night, didn't you?" he asked as an afterthought.

"Yes, but the Ziploc bag wasn't there this morning. The people who come in to clean on Wednesday night must have thought it was trash and threw it away."

"No big deal," he said. "It wasn't anything we could take to the D.A."

"Ah, yes, but I have good news for you. I found a few more samples of the hair by going through the clothes this morning before we cleaned them. They're waiting in our lost-and-found drawer for you back at the plant at this very moment."

"Great." I could tell his heart wasn't in it, but he said he would try to stop by the cleaners later to pick up the packet. Maybe he'd ask me out for dinner again, and this time I was free. At least until ten o'clock, when Nat and I had rescheduled our dinner date.

I watched the social worker fill out the paperwork on Betty.

"Her clothes were all bloody when she arrived," she said tactfully, not mentioning the Hefty bag. "You might want to bring her some fresh things to wear."

"Sure. I can do that." After all, we still had a few Christmas donations coming in for the homeless shelter.

I thanked her for her help and headed back for the cleaners before I hooked up with the rational part of my being again.

Business was booming when I came into the call office. It was probably because the weather had improved and people wanted to get out before the next storm, predicted for tonight.

I pulled off my suit jacket, tossed it on the marking table, and prepared to go to work. Ordinarily we attempted to get each customer in and out in two minutes, but today they were stacked up like sweaters on a President's Day sales table at Foley's.

Lucille was out front, too, and she wasn't happy about it. "It's been a zoo ever since you left," she complained. "Ann Marie had to leave early because of a dental appointment."

I told Lucille to go back to the marking table and took over for her on the counter. By three o'clock things were back to normal, but there would be another rush when people got off work tonight. Picking up clothes for a big weekend, probably, which reminded me that I should have brought in my "basic black" to have it cleaned just in case I didn't get to the mall and needed a backup dress for David's party tomorrow. Too late for that.

I grabbed a handful of messages off my spindle on the marking table. While-you-were-out notes for calls I needed to return and names of people I had to get in touch with because there was a problem with their clothes.

If customers weren't happy with their clothes, we gave them the orders free or offered to redo them, but sometimes Mack would have left me a note that he couldn't get a spot out without resorting to desperate measures that might ruin the fabric. Things like iodine and photographic chemicals are the devil to get out of clothes, and in such cases I call the customer and get an okay from them before we do anything more.

I hadn't even finished the calls to customers about the burglary, so I closed the door to the office, determined to spend the next few hours on the phone. I reviewed the messages before I set to work, skimming over one that Ann Marie had written that morning. Whoa! Back up. I flipped through the pages I'd just read. In her round teenage script Ann Marie had written, "Eric J. asked if he brot in a jgg'g suit. He can't find it, but we have no rc'd of it."

First I had to translate her abbreviations. Wouldn't you know she'd abbreviate the important words? Eric Jenkins? Jogging suit? No record of it?

It sounded just like Eric to have a jogging suit that he had to send to the cleaners. He'd probably paid more for it than I could afford for the after-five dress I needed to buy. It was no longer a priority. Eric's jgg'g suit was.

Maybe it had been in the clothes the police confiscated from our pickup closet at O'Brien and Van Dyke. However, Foster had said he checked with our customers about all the clothes that had been dumped on the closet floor, and they'd said nothing was missing. But as I'd told him, it wasn't uncommon for customers to forget what they sent to us. Now that we had the computer, it could keep track of the clothes and generate letters to people who hadn't picked up their clothes for six weeks. However, it was particularly confusing for customers like Eric, who brought some clothes to the cleaners himself and used our pickup service for others.

But what if . . . ? I plugged in the computer and looked at his recent orders. He'd picked up an order on Monday, and when he was in the next day, he'd picked up the order that had been scheduled for delivery. No jogging suit among the clothes. I jumped up from the desk and sailed through the plant to Lucille at the marking table.

I waved the memo at her. "Ann Marie said Eric Jenkins was in this morning looking for a jogging suit he thought he might have brought in," I said. "Do you know anything about it?"

"Ann Marie *was* back here looking for something," Lucille said disinterestedly as she kept marking in the clothes. "I told her to look at that rack where we put stuff that doesn't have a ticket on it. She didn't find anything."

We have all sorts of cross-checks on garments, and we note the color on our computer and whether the fabric is checked or plaid or polka dot. If we don't do that and an item gets separated from its mates, despite every precaution we take, we have a rack that we put the orphans on.

"Did she mention what color it was?"

"No, when she went back out to ask some more questions about it, she said the guy had taken off like he had ants in his pants."

A distressing visual picture for a cleaners, and puzzling besides. I took a look at our no-name rail. There were only a couple of items on it and definitely no jogging suit.

I was so excited I went back to Mack and hung over his spotting board, forcing him to turn off his spray gun.

"I think I'm onto something," I said. "The attorney we saw in Tico Taco's came in here today looking for a jogging suit, but we don't have it." I paused for the dramatic emphasis that Mack's so big on. "I bet it's the outfit the killer took out of our delivery closet to wear after he murdered Harrison Van Dyke."

"Why do you say that?" Mack asked.

I didn't want to go into the way Eric had left the counter

in such a hurry. "Just a hunch," I said, "but I'm going to call the customer right now and check it out."

"Let me know what you find out." Mack turned back to the spotting board.

"Oh, by the way," I said, as if it were going to be only a slight stain on the fabric of my life, "I invited Betty to come and stay with me until this thing is over."

"You did what?" His voice resonated around the plant.

I thought after I'd fed him such a tasty bit of gossip about the jogging suit, he would have taken my other news more graciously. "I invited . . ." I started to repeat.

"I know what you said. You got no business getting more messed up in this than you are already. She'd be safer someplace else than with you."

"But you're the one who said, and I quote, she's mad as hell and she ain't going to take it anymore." With that I beat a quick retreat to my office, stopping only to add, "That was Peter Finch in the movie *Network*, by the way."

As soon as I reached the desk, I tried calling Eric at the law firm. Things must be back to normal because Ms. Sexy Voice answered the phone and told me in a sultry whisper that he was in court and wouldn't be back today. I declined to leave a message, not wanting to tip my hand that I was calling about the jogging suit.

I called Ann Marie, but there was no answer, so I worked my way through a lot of the other calls I needed to make, mostly leaving messages on people's answering machines.

Finally I tried Ann Marie again. Her private line, like so many kids have nowadays, was busy. She probably had a beeper, but I didn't know the number, and at least I knew she was home. I reached her just before I had to go back up front and help my evening counter crew with the five o'clock rush.

"What's this note about Eric Jenkins losing a jogging suit?" I asked when I finally got through to her.

"I couldn't find it, but he was so, like really anxious to locate it that I went in back to take one more look, and when I came out to the counter again, he was gone. Julia had been waiting on another customer, and he told her to tell me to forget it. He'd just had an idea what might have happened to it."

"Did he say what color it was?" I thought maybe I'd take one more look around the plant to make sure it wasn't here. The best way to do that when something's lost is to eyeball for color.

"I think he said it was something like, you know, 'Sahara sunset' or 'sand dune'—like that."

"And what, pray tell, does that mean?" I asked.

Ann Marie was silent for a minute, as if I had sprung a pop quiz on her. "I'm, you know, not exactly sure," she said.

I asked her if Eric had said anything else about the suit. She said no, and I hung up before she could spring another "you know" on me.

I vowed to have a session with my employees on speaking basic color-wheel English, not colors according to designer labels. Still, I had to admit that only a person like Eric with an expensive jogging suit would describe it as "Sahara sunset" or—like that. I'm surprised he didn't say it was "puce" or "burnt sienna," something that only us artsy-types would know, although puce was probably too ugly-sounding to go with the care label on designer sportswear.

With a pair of sweats from a discount store, "Sahara sunset" would be just plain tan or pink or maybe orange.

I'd take one more look around the plant for a stray jogging suit in an earth tone, I decided. If I couldn't find it, I'd share my suspicions with Foster as soon as he showed up.

Wouldn't he be surprised? Oh, by the way, I'd say, I may have figured out what the killer was wearing when he made his escape from the O'Brien and Van Dyke offices. He'd be so pleased that he'd surely issue me a commendation or that dinner invitation.

I went up front to help with the after-work rush.

It came and went without any visits from the police. So much for my fantasy about a filet with Foster.

But never let it be said that I don't bounce back. I like to think I'm kind of like spandex. If he wasn't going to show, why didn't I try calling Eric again?

I looked up his number and dialed the phone. He answered on the second ring, just as I was in the process of formulating a plan. Unfortunately I didn't have it all worked out.

"Oh, hi, Eric. This is Mandy Dyer." And suddenly an idea came to me. "I think we found your jogging suit." I'd been lying so much lately that some mental antihistamine must have kicked in. I didn't even itch.

"Really?" He sounded surprised. "Are you sure?"

"Well, I can't be positive. There's no ticket on it, but I was wondering if you wanted to stop by tomorrow morning to see about it. Since we've inconvenienced you, there won't be any charge for the cleaning."

"Uh—I'll be in court tomorrow. Any chance you could bring it over to my place tonight?"

I hadn't expected that, but it certainly indicated that he

hadn't found the jogging suit. I had to make a quick deci-
sion. Nat's "very reliable source" had said Eric had an alibi
for the time of the murder, so I decided to go with that.

"Okay," I agreed.

"I have to go someplace at eight-thirty tonight, so the
sooner you can get here the better," Eric said. "I'll make it
worth your while."

CHAPTER
20

Now that I'd told Eric we had his jogging suit, I had to deliver. I gazed around the cleaning plant in dismay, wondering if I could find some other customer's jogging suit to "borrow." That seemed like a bad policy. What if Eric claimed it? Finally, I went over to our Christmas donation box and started digging through it. I found a mustard-colored sweatsuit that was a little the worse for wear. Close enough. What did I know about a Sahara sunset anyway? I put it on a hanger and bagged it.

It wasn't until I was in the van that I began to hone in on the problem of delivering the suit personally. Was I out of my mind to go see a guy who, only hours before, I'd thought was a prime suspect in Van Dyke's murder? With a sweatsuit that I already knew wasn't his?

Quit worrying about it, I told myself as I wound my way to Leetsdale Drive and picked up Alameda going east. Hadn't Nat's source said Eric had an alibi. He has an alibi, he has an alibi, I repeated like a mantra.

Once I calmed myself down about that, I began to think

about Eric's parting shot, "I'll make it worth your while. . . ." Oh, please, no sexy come-ons, Eric. But I could handle any suggestive remarks or sexual innuendos. Just not murderers.

What I needed to do was concentrate on his jogging suit. Did Eric think it had something to do with the killer? When he rejected the garment I was bringing him, I figured, I'd be able to question him about it.

He'd given me directions to his townhouse, which was in Aurora, a suburb of Denver. By the time I got there, I thought I was halfway to Kansas or the new Denver International Airport, whichever came first.

The moon had been out when I left the office, but it was hidden behind clouds by the time I reached the development, which was called Coventry Gardens. From what I could see in the headlights of the van, the place looked neither English nor lush with plants.

I drove through the mazelike streets, but somewhere I must have taken a wrong turn. I wound up back at the main gate. I tried again and eventually found a map that looked like a you-are-here diagram in a shopping mall. It told me how to get to Building F, Unit 32, which was the address Eric had given me.

When I reached it, the adjoining unit was dark, but I could see a light in a front window of Eric's place. Finding the entrance was another matter. It was tucked away on the opposite side of the two-story building from F34, I presume to provide privacy for the comings and goings of the respective residents. Eric's BMW, the one Ann Marie had thought was awesome, was in front of his place, but parked so far out in the street that it was as if he'd decided the walk to the curb would do him good.

A north wind blew across the sidewalk as I got out of the van. I grabbed the garment bag with the bogus sweatsuit in it and hurried to the side of the house. The wind was the harbinger of another cold front that was predicted to move through Colorado tonight. I had changed into jeans and a trench coat I'd retrieved from my summer wardrobe yesterday.

The coat replaced the down jacket I'd gotten blood on when I found Betty. I'd given it our best water-repellent treatment when I'd had it cleaned earlier in the fall, but that didn't help much in this kind of weather. I pulled the coat collar up around my neck, the fact not lost on me that I looked a little like one of the thirties detectives in those Hammett-Chandler novels I enjoyed so much. Except I was female. I kind of liked it.

The light from a distant streetlamp faded as I rounded the corner of the building, and I nearly tripped over an outcropping of low bushes. Once I righted myself, I made my way to a porch that was roughly the size of my kitchen table. I could see the step up to the porch because light filtered out from where the front door was cracked open. I could hear Ravel's *Bolero* playing on a stereo inside. Oh, please, not that!

Wasn't that what Bo Derek had proclaimed as the music-to-have-sex-by in that old movie with Dudley Moore? I'd have to ask Mack what the name of the movie was. At least the music didn't conjure up a picture of a murderer, and as long as Eric didn't show up naked with an unlit cigarette behind his ear, I was sure I could handle the situation. In fact the image made me laugh, and I decided this was just Eric's idea of a joke.

He must have left the door ajar so that he could hear

me over the music when I arrived. I rang the doorbell and counted to ten. That was the name of the movie—*10*. I was pleased with the way my subconscious mind worked.

The bell was working, too, because I could hear it peal, but Eric didn't answer.

I doubled up my fist and knocked on the door. It opened easily on its well-oiled hinges to give me an unobstructed view of the entrance hall. Unfortunately I couldn't see anything else. Just my luck this wasn't one of those free-flowing architectural designs. The light was coming through a door to the right, like a spot being cast down on a stage but fading to black as a stairway swept up into the darkness of a second story.

I thought about turning around and leaving, but damn it, no guy playing *Bolero* on his stereo was going to scare me away.

"Eric," I yelled so my voice would carry to the upper level, where he probably was getting ready for his eight-thirty appointment. "It's me, Mandy, with your dry-cleaning order."

No answer.

I stepped over the threshold to the ceramic-tiled floor. There was a closed door on one side, probably a closet, and a wooden display case on the other side with some statues on it. I wondered briefly if they were a collection of lewd nudes. Or maybe they were trophies for being Lawyer of the Year. In cleaning circles people mostly received plaques.

As I walked past the case, I could see an open area to the left with enough light shining across from the opposite side of the hall to tell me it was the living room.

I was almost to the door where the light was coming from when the whole place went dark. I couldn't see a thing. This was no place for a dry cleaner. I turned and started back to the entrance. I'd almost made it when someone slammed into me from behind, nearly knocking me down and sending the garment bag flying out of my hand.

So much for Eric having an alibi. This was no jumping-the-bones attack. Had he been lying in wait for me because he thought I knew too much?

He grabbed me around the waist, pinning my arms to my sides. I flailed to get out of his grip. It didn't work. I kicked with my foot, hitting a shin ineffectually with one of my sneakers.

"Stop it, Eric," I screamed.

The only thing I could think of was that I was going to be stabbed, just the way Van Dyke and Betty had been. I had to get away without giving him a chance to free up a hand so he could plunge a knife into me.

He was still holding on with both arms, but we were caught in a kind of weird dance in which we pirouetted around drunkenly in a circle with him attached to my back. I tried to bend down and pitch him over my shoulder. It didn't work. We both plowed into the case of statues, sending them skittering on their sides. I reached out to steady myself while I tried to shake him off and managed to grab one of the statues as it started to roll off a table.

I got a grip on what felt like the ankles of an Oscar-like trophy. Now, if I could just use it as a weapon. The guy clung to me like static electricity. I twisted one of my legs behind me to try to trip him. We fell to the floor, and the fall loosened his hold on me. I started to crawl away from him, using the statue in my hand like a machete to whack away at him.

I heard a howl and knew I'd hit him. He scrambled after me, his face just a dark outline as my eyes began to adjust to the faint light coming through the open front door. He was grabbing at my legs, pursuing me like a giant crab. I twisted around and kicked him.

"Let go, you bastard," I screamed. I leaned toward him and tried to land another blow. Big mistake. He hit me on the forehead with something, and my head banged against the floor.

I lay there stunned, my head swimming as if I were in five feet of water. I must have lost consciousness for a few seconds because when I came to, he was dragging me across the floor. He lifted me and then dropped me on top of some objects I couldn't identify. I played dead as my face landed in something that smelled like a dirty laundry hamper. A door slammed against my feet, and everything went black.

Or had I passed out again? No, I could hear something being dragged across the floor on the other side of the door. I realized the music had stopped. I could heard someone grunt. Another door slammed. Seconds ticked by. Somewhere a car started and drove away.

Still I didn't move. I hardly breathed. When I did, all I could smell was sweat. I waited until I could no longer hear the car, then felt around with my hands to see what was in my face. I hadn't been far wrong about the odor. I decided I had my nose buried in Eric's gym bag, and I had the headache from hell.

I lifted myself up slowly, careful not to make any sudden

movements. There were shoes everywhere. I must be in the closet just off the entry.

Pushing the shoes aside to make a space for myself, I sat up and took a gulp of air. Something slapped over my lips like a suction cup. I was suffocating. Surely there wasn't someone in the closet with me. I spat the thing out of my mouth and swatted in front of me. It was a plastic garment bag like we dry cleaners use. I started to laugh; I was on the verge of hysteria.

Calm down, I told myself. I fought off a wave of claustrophobia as I patted around on my body. No obvious stab wounds. I touched my forehead. There was a knot at the hairline, and I had to bite my lip to keep from letting out a yelp of pain.

I sat motionless, listening. As the silence grew, I became convinced my attacker was gone. After all, he could have killed me while he had the chance instead of throwing me in the closet.

So why hadn't he killed me? If it was Eric, wouldn't he have killed me rather than leave me alive to tell the police he'd murdered Van Dyke? But could Eric have been dumb enough to come to the cleaners this morning about a jogging suit that he suddenly remembered he'd grabbed from his own dirty clothes bag the night he killed Van Dyke? It didn't seem likely.

The only other possibility was that I'd surprised someone who'd broken into Eric's house. I hadn't thought to look at my watch when I arrived. Maybe it had taken me longer to find his place than I'd thought and Eric hadn't been able to wait for me.

Either way I had to get out of the closet. I reached up and

grabbed the doorknob. It turned, but the door wouldn't open. The bastard had jammed something up against it, so I was trapped inside. I squeezed my way up through the clothes, dislodging hangers as I went, and pushed with my shoulder against the door.

"Oh, God." A sharp pain shot through me from where I must have bruised the shoulder in the fight.

I retreated to the floor and cleared more shoes and the hangers out of the way. I put my back against the door and my feet against the opposite wall and started pushing again. It was awkward because I had to hold one hand over my head to retract the latch mechanism on the doorknob.

"Push, damn it, push." I sounded like a Lamaze coach.

The door moved a little. I no longer needed to twist the knob. I pushed harder. The door gave way, toppling whatever had been holding it shut. The crash sounded like an explosion. I fell out of the closet, hitting my head on the tile and sending laser beams of pain to my brain.

When the pain subsided, I got up and banged into the thing that had trapped me inside. I could feel by the shape of it that it was the display case, its glass shelves now shattered on the floor. My shoes crunched on the broken shards as I tried to move around the heavy piece of furniture toward the front door. The display case had fallen against it, blocking my exit from the building. I changed directions. As I did, I kicked one of the statues and groped on the floor to pick it up. Just in case.

I felt my way along the wall to where I'd seen the light shining out from the other room and fumbled for a wall switch. I flipped it on, and the statue fell out of my hand.

There was no attacker waiting for me here. Just Eric. He was lying on the kitchen floor wearing one of the freshly starched shirts we'd probably laundered and pressed for him a few days before. It was covered with blood.

CHAPTER 21

I stared at Eric in horror and disbelief. I'd had this awful feeling all along that the person who hit me over the head was the same person who'd killed Van Dyke and tried to kill Betty, but I'd thought it was Eric. So who was it?

I bent down and retrieved the statue from the floor, suddenly afraid the real killer was still lurking somewhere in the house. I stopped and listened. Nothing.

With the statue clutched in my hands like a club, I forced myself to go over to where Eric lay on the floor. His eyes stared up at me in surprise. His mouth gaped open. I knelt beside him. Maybe he was still alive, I told myself, the way Betty had been.

"Eric," I whispered, but without any real hope. At least Betty had groaned.

I tried to find a pulse on his neck. I couldn't feel one. I tried his wrist. Still nothing. I was going to be sick, but I staggered to the phone. I'd be damned if I'd be sick before I called for help.

I swallowed hard and told a dispatcher that there'd been a

murder. I don't know how I remembered the address but I did. "Building F, Unit thirty-two," I said.

I hoped to God the cops wouldn't have as hard a time finding the place as I'd had. I was incapable of giving directions or even telling them how to find the you-are-here map.

"Stay on the phone," the dispatcher instructed.

"Okay," I said. No need to hang up the way I had with Betty.

I had the phone clutched in one hand and the statue in the other. I looked down at the figure on its heavy base. It wasn't a nude at all but a small bronze sculpture of a cowboy by a local artist. Go figure. I never would have taken Eric for an art lover, and somehow it seemed unbearably sad that I'd never known that about him.

"I'll be back," I said into the phone. "I have to throw up."

Detective Foster didn't show up at Eric's townhouse. Aurora was out of his jurisdiction, and another set of cops responded to the call.

But Nat arrived about half an hour after the APD homicide unit. As a roving reporter, he covers a much wider territory than Foster. He probably heard the call over the police scanner at the *Trib* and came tearing out here, all thoughts of our dinner forgotten, as he raced to the site of another homicide.

Before his arrival I'd been grilled by a heavyset detective named Lucero, who looked like a pit bull; checked out by a paramedic, who said I probably only had a mild concussion; and left by myself on a brown leather sofa in the living room with nothing to do but stare at a painting on the adjacent wall.

It was a scene of the Rockies, denuded of trees and devoid of snow. The painting of the barren mountain peaks must have been chosen to go with the color scheme, not for any artistic merit. Besides, where was the snow?

While I pondered the question, I overheard one of the policemen in the kitchen say Eric had been shot to death. All I'd noticed was the blood.

Suddenly there was a racket at the front door, and I sat up straighter on the sofa. Nat flashed his press card at a policeman at the door and forced his way inside before the young cop could stop him. He was wearing jeans and a yellow sweatshirt under his black leather jacket, and he had on a black safety helmet with a yellow racing stripe across the top. The outfit made him look like a giant bumblebee.

"Thank God, Mandy," he said when he spotted me. "I was afraid it was you when I saw that stupid fresh-as-a-daisy van outside." He took off his helmet and headed toward me. "You were supposed to be home waiting for me to get off work so we could go to dinner."

Well, that did it. Maybe he was concerned about my welfare, but the way he expected me to be sitting at home while he was off on the trail of another story set me off. His crack about our logo didn't help either. He could have at least noticed the ugly welt on my forehead, but once he found out I wasn't dead, that's all he cared about.

"Excuse me," I said, "but if I'd been waiting for you, I'd have been out of luck, wouldn't I?"

And for that matter, I fumed inwardly, if he were such a good friend, why *wasn't* he at my apartment right now, worrying and fretting about where I was, not out in hot pursuit of another story?

"Hey, whoa, partner." Nat dropped down on the sofa beside me. "Start at the beginning and tell your old buddy Nat what happened?"

"Not bloody likely." I shuddered at the words which sounded as if I'd been hanging around Betty too long.

He finally noticed the bruise on my forehead. "What's that bump on your—?"

Before he could finish, Detective Lucero came charging across the hall from the kitchen. "Oh, it's you, Wilcox," he snarled. "Don't talk to our witness until we're through with her."

Nat gave my arm what he probably thought was a reassuring squeeze and got up. "Okay, okay, Lucero," he said, raising his hands in the air as he backed away. "I'm glad you're okay, Mandy, and we'll talk later. Okay?"

Always the reporter, he went for his notebook and pen as he turned to Lucero, ready to get a few good quotes that the rest of the press corps wasn't privy to. Then Lucero threw him out, and he had to join the other reporters outside on the lawn.

They'd swarmed around the townhouse like locusts as soon as the news went out. Through one of the living-room windows I could see the lights of the camcorders from the TV news teams, and the occasional flash of a still camera as the print media vied for the story.

I was left to wonder at my angry reaction to Nat. After all, he was my best friend, and I already knew how infuriating he could be. Why should I be surprised that he'd shown up here instead of on my doorstep?

I returned to staring at the painting, and it was only then that I noticed the naked lady hidden in one of the rock formations. It was like one of those drawings for kids: "Find ten animal friends in this picture." I discovered another nude figure farther up on the mountain. No wonder there was no snow. This was a flesh-toned painting. Poor old Eric. No art lover, after all.

Lucero came back in the living room and insisted on going over my statement again. He seemed skeptical of my story about the jogging suit and how I thought Eric's death was connected to the Van Dyke murder.

Finally he said I could go and offered to have someone drive me to the hospital in case I needed more medical attention.

I declined. "I want to go home." I sounded like a petulant five-year-old, and I hated that. I tried for a more mature voice. "Really, I appreciate the offer, but I'm feeling all right now." Sure I was.

"Okay, you're free to go, but we'll need to talk to you later," he said, verifying both my work and home addresses. "I'll have someone escort you to your car."

He had a young guy in uniform take me out a back door and around the townhouse to the van to avoid the press. One of the reporters broke away from the media mob and hurried to the van. It was Nat of course.

"I'll drive her home, officer," he said, then looked at me. "Lucero said you were hit over the head. You probably shouldn't drive."

Okay, I was adult enough that I could accept help when I needed it. Who cared whether Nat was doing it for humanitarian reasons or because he wanted a scoop from the eyewitness? It didn't matter. My brain felt as if it had been squashed in one of our hothead presses and steam was coming out my ears.

I climbed into the passenger's seat of the van. "Thanks," I said, my way of apologizing for my earlier anger at him. "What are you going to do with the Harley? Just leave it here?"

"Of course not." He looked over at me and winked. "Do you think I'd offer to drive you home if you didn't have a van? I'll just put it in the back."

I seethed. "I should have known better."

Never let a guy escort you home if he has to stow a Harley in back. By the time Nat got through bouncing the van around, trying to batten down the motorcycle, I was grimacing in pain.

He finally got around to ooohing over the knot on my forehead and insisted that we stop at the ER at Rose Medical Center en route to my place. We found out what I already knew—that I had a slight concussion and the headache from hell. The Emergency Room doctor gave me some pain pills and told me to see my own doctor if I didn't feel better in the morning.

"Hey, I'm sorry I was ticked off at you earlier," Nat said when we were back in the van.

"*You* were ticked off at *me*?"

"Yeah, I was so damned scared when I spotted the van, but then I saw you sitting there in the living room, all cool and collected, and I could have wrung your neck."

How could I stay mad at a guy who didn't even know I was mad at him in the first place?

"Apologies accepted," I said, and let it go at that.

He nodded as he squinted through his wire-rimmed glasses at the road. "Next time you go out looking for trouble, I want to be with you."

I leaned my head back and closed my eyes. "You're only

saying that because you want to be the first one on the scene."

"So why'd you go out there?" Nat asked.

I told him about Eric's missing jogging suit and how I'd gone there to find out if it could have been what the killer wore when he left the murder scene Monday morning. "I think Eric figured out something about the suit when he was at the cleaners," I explained. "Lucille said he went tearing out of there like a guy with 'ants in his pants.' "

"How'd you get inside Eric's place?"

"The door was open, and at first I thought the police were going to arrest me for entering an 'unsecured domicile,' as one of the policemen put it."

Nat laughed. "Oh, yes, the old unsecured-domicile ploy." He sounded like Mack imitating W. C. Fields.

I opened one eye to look at him and could tell we were almost home. It was a relief because riding with Nat was always risky. His night vision left something to be desired.

There was a parking space right in front of my apartment. My lucky day. Nat came upstairs with me and insisted on getting me settled on the couch. Spot pouted by his food dish until he was fed. Thank God, Nat was there to bend down and put food in the dish. I didn't think my head would have allowed for any more on-the-floor gymnastics.

Then Nat buzzed around and fixed an ice pack for my head. He followed that up by making dinner out of what he could find in my understocked refrigerator. Eggs and cheese would have to do.

"I'm impressed that you'd do this instead of calling in your story," I said as he slipped an omelet from the frying pan onto a plate and brought it over to the coffee table.

"No problem," he said. "I called in the story on the cell phone. They could only use a couple of graphs, and I'll fill in the details tomorrow."

Nat went back and fixed his own omelet, then plopped down in a lotus position on the floor at my feet. "After the guy who killed Jenkins hit you over the head, were you out cold for a while or what?"

I guess I wanted sympathy. I told him how my attacker had tossed me in a closet as if I were an old coat and how I'd wound up having to fight my way out of a stinking gym bag and through a bunch of clothes, not to mention the poly bag that I'd thought was someone trying to suffocate me.

"I hope it wasn't a Dyer's Cleaners bag," he said. Apparently he found that more amusing than I did, because he started to laugh.

Yeah, I could just see Nat's headline—CLEANER ASPHYXI-ATED BY OWN PLASTIC BAG. I started to laugh, too, but only because Nat affects me that way. "Please don't do that," I said.

"Do what?" He lifted his glasses to wipe his eyes.

"Don't make me laugh. It hurts." Now I knew how Betty had felt in the hospital yesterday morning.

"I'm sorry," he said, trying to put on a solemn face. Finally he bounced up to clear the plates off the coffee table. "I just—" He started to laugh again. "I just keep having this mental picture of the cleaner locked in the clothes closet."

I put the ice pack back on my head, sorry that I'd told him the story at all. "You have to understand," I said, "that was before I knew about Eric. It was awful finding. . ."

Nat looked contrite. "I know, Mandy." He came back over, sat down beside me, and put his arm around me.

"It was so terrible finding him lying there, and I didn't

even know he'd been shot. I thought he'd been stabbed." I was on a teeter-totter ride with my emotions, and I suddenly started to blink back tears.

Nat patted me on the shoulder. "It's okay," he said. "It's okay to cry."

That's what he'd told me when Larry the Law Student dumped me and a few months later when Uncle Chet died. When Nat had told me the same thing in high school after Mom married a guy I hated, I'd thought I was too old to cry. Fortunately Nat had helped me outgrow my feelings about showing my emotions, and he might not be very dependable for dates, but he was dynamite when I really needed him.

No way could I stay mad at a guy like that, but I didn't dare let go this time, because it hurt too much to cry. I sniffled for a few minutes, but finally got control of myself.

Nat offered the opinion that instead of thinking about what happened, we ought to try to figure out why it happened.

I decided to tell him about the hairs we'd found on Van Dyke's clothes. When I was almost through, I let out a hiccup as an aftereffect of the suppressed tears. "Oh, damn, I'm not going to start that." Between the itching when I lied and the hiccups when I cried, I was a walking barometer of mood swings. It was particularly irritating this time because every hiccup was punctuated with a piercing pain to my temple.

Nat went to get me a spoonful of sugar and told me to swallow it slowly. It helped, and I held my breath while Nat carried the ball for a while.

"So you think maybe Pamela Leyton, the blond receptionist, was having an affair with Van Dyke, and he dumped her for a brunette?" he concluded.

I nodded.

"Well, maybe she killed Van Dyke, and Eric knew about it. Pamela could have killed Eric because she thought he was going to squeal on her."

"But I think the person who attacked me was a man." I stopped for a minute to see if I was going to hiccup again. I didn't. "I'm sure it was a man," I continued, curling up on one end of the sofa with the ice bag still plopped on my head like a beret.

"So I wonder if the cops know anything about this brunette you're telling me about," Nat said.

"I'm not sure. Foster won't tell me a thing, but I keep thinking it might be someone named Margaret. I told you about hearing Pamela and Eric talking in Tico Taco's the other night, and I heard her say something nasty about a woman named Margaret, as if she'd replaced Pamela as Van Dyke's lover."

Nat slipped back down on the floor and pulled out his notebook. "Maybe we should start some kind of flow chart. Remember, you said the other day that if Betty didn't see the guy who tossed the suit in the trash can, then someone could have heard about her that day in the law office when you were telling the cops about her? But hadn't the story about Betty already been released by the time she was stabbed?"

"Yes, but she said someone tried to run her down Monday too. The killer had to know about her even before the story came out and been afraid she could identify him."

"Okay, so who was in the law firm who could have heard you talking about Betty?"

"Pamela was the only one, but I suppose she could have told some of the other people."

Nat fidgeted on the floor. "See, we're back to her again."

"But that's the trouble. Foster doesn't think she over- heard enough of the conversation to make any sense of it."

Just then I heard a bang, and I jumped with a start. It was only Spot, making a four-point landing on the floor after a covert action up on the kitchen counter. Too late to repri- mand the sneaky devil, who'd taken unfair advantage of my weakened condition.

I shrugged my bruised shoulder and decided to ig- nore him.

"You also thought someone could have seen her at the trash can and followed her to the cleaners."

I nodded. "That's another reason I thought Eric was such a good suspect. He came in right after she left."

"But now Eric's dead," Nat said. As if he had to remind me.

We both watched as Spot skulked away from the kitchen and headed behind some of my paintings, which were leaning against a wall in a far corner of the room. He knew he'd done something he wasn't supposed to do.

"The only other thing I can think of . . ." I stopped and stiffened. "No, it's too dumb even to mention."

"What?" Nat doodled on a page of his notebook, but his artwork wasn't nearly as good as mine. "Go ahead. We're just brainstorming right now."

"Well, the only other place I can think of where someone could have found out about Betty is inside the cleaners. Oh, but that's impossible."

"Why?"

I frowned at him. "Because I don't want it to be "

Nat tapped his pen on the notebook. "But that's a really

interesting possibility. It could have been someone who was already there when Betty came in."

Suddenly I bolted upright. "There was someone. She's the manager of a fancy dress store in the neighborhood. Her name is Maggie."

"Margaret . . ." Nat said.

CHAPTER 22

I told Nat I didn't know anything about Maggie, really, except that she was a brunette and she dressed well. Her hair was straighter than what I'd found on Van Dyke's clothes, but maybe she kinked it up for the kinky sex on V.D.'s Navajo rugs.

What I didn't know I aimed to find out, and what better way to do it than to go shopping at the high-fashion dress salon where she worked. After all, I needed a fancy dress for the party I was scheduled to go to with David the next night.

I glanced at my watch. Oh, great. It was after midnight so it was already Friday. And before I did anything else, I would have to go to the hospital to spring Betty from her enforced confinement. That was going to be fun.

Nat laughed himself silly when I told him I was bringing her home, but to his credit he didn't disapprove. He was the only person I knew who didn't think it was a crazy idea.

"Good for you," he said. "And to think I was afraid you'd change when you took over Uncle Chet's business."

"Thanks loads."

At the time, he was pulling out the rollaway bed I kept for guests, mainly my mother. I knew Mom hated it, so she always opted to go to a hotel when she came to Denver. I myself slept on the sofa bed I'd been lying on all evening, but tonight I decided not to bother pulling out the Hide-A-Bed.

"You always were a sucker for strays," Nat said.

He'd insisted on spending the night to make sure I was all right. He'd turned off the lights and fell onto the rollaway fully clothed. I swear that's the way he probably sleeps half the time at home. Always ready on a moment's notice to respond to a crime anywhere in the Denver metropolitan area.

"Remember when we were kids," he said through the darkness, "and we found that lost kitten at the tennis court? You dragged it home, but your stepdad wouldn't let you keep it."

"Yeah, old Anthony the Hun." I was referring to my stepfather, not the cat.

"And you made a real pain of yourself at school asking people to take the kitten."

"Actually I was trying to get someone to take Tony," I said. "I was glad when Mom divorced him."

"It took you a whole week to find someone stupid enough to take the cat."

"*You* took the cat."

"Like I said . . ."

"Hey, you wouldn't like another feline friend, would you?"

"You know you wouldn't part with Spot."

"Yeah, the cat who never met a person he didn't dislike."

I think Nat kept talking, but I drifted off to sleep, unaware that Spot's personality was about to undergo a metamorphic change.

Betty came to a dead stop the minute she walked inside my apartment. I'd have thought she'd seen the killer except that she was staring straight at Spot.

"I hate cats," she said, putting her hands to the bodice of the blue pants suit I'd found for her in our used clothing box. I'd had to stop and buy her some underwear, which I hoped fit better than the suit. It was a little large for her. Who'd have guessed she was that skinny under all those layers of clothes? Still, the suit didn't look bad, considering the fact that she had insisted on wearing it above her old combat boots.

I nudged her into the room. "It's okay," I said. "Spot hates people, so it should work out just fine."

Little did I know. Spot, sensing that Betty didn't care for him, took her disdain as a challenge. I wouldn't go so far as to say he took a liking to her, but as cats are wont to do, once he sensed her fear, he decided to ingratiate himself with her. He came over and wound himself around her legs.

"Shoo," she said, stomping her boots and waving her hand at him to scare him away.

Spot was unperturbed. He'd finally found the person he'd been waiting for all his life. Someone who didn't like him. "Get away," Betty said. "Scat."

I told her to go have a seat in the overstuffed chair over in the conversational grouping of furniture that marked out my living room. I said I'd feed the beast and then he'd be okay.

But as God is my witness, Spot jumped up on the arm of the chair and began to circle her as if he were getting ready for the kill. Up on the back of the chair, down the other arm, across her lap. Back on the arm of the chair, up, down. Betty gripped the chair like a white-knuckle flyer buckled into her seat for takeoff. This wasn't going to work.

Finally when Spot had completed his second circle and jumped on the back of the chair again, Betty launched herself up and made her escape. "I know you mean well, Princess, but I think I better be movin' along."

"No, Betty. That isn't an option. You aren't leaving until the killer is found."

Spot eyed her happily, as if she were a large mouse.

I sighed. "I'll take Spot to work with me, okay?"

It wasn't as if he hadn't been there before. After all, he used to be the resident cat at the cleaners. For all I knew, he might even enjoy a return to his former home.

"Ohhh—kay," she said, staring at him suspiciously.

I actually hadn't been feeling too bad this morning. Until I tried to corral the cat.

I went over to a walk-in closet off the living room. It was so large I'd even considered turning it into my bedroom, but it didn't have any windows, and after being locked up last night, I wasn't even sure I liked it as a closet. It had become the resting-place for everything I owned, from art supplies and large canvases I'd painted during my manic post-Larry period to clothes and the other debris of normal living. It was a mess, and I realized I shouldn't have cussed out Eric's closet so much. Mine was just as bad, although it smelled better. Linseed oil instead of sweat.

I'd read about a dry cleaner in Nebraska who also ran a closet shop, one of those places that has all sorts of closet organizers, shoe bags, and quilted hangers. Maybe I should start a business like that as a sideline to my cleaners. From closets I'd seen recently, there were a lot of people who could use the help. I'd have to give it some thought when I had the time.

I plowed through the stuff on the floor, digging back into the junk until I finally found the cat carrier. It was called a Cat Taxi, and Spot still remembered it. He took one look at the barred cage and took off, escaping to his hiding place behind my after-the-depression artwork in a corner of the main room. Maybe the carrier was enough of a scare that, if I left it here in the middle of the floor, it would keep him away from Betty.

I couldn't risk it. He was a sneaky creature, and the moment I left, he'd know the threat was over and come sneaking out to terrorize my guest. I opened the cage door so I'd be ready for him, then pulled the canvases down in one quick movement and laid them on the floor. Spot raced out from his hiding place, knocking over the easel where I had an unfinished painting. My latest work-in-progress was a swirl of spring colors, meant to signify the return to a more tranquil period in my life. Yeah, right. No wonder I hadn't been able to finish it.

Spot meanwhile had escaped behind the sofa bed. I opened a can of the feline junk food for him. I finally lured him out from behind the sofa enough that I could grab him by the nape of his neck.

"Gotcha," I said triumphantly.

"Gotcha," Spot proclaimed in action, not words. He slashed his claws across the back of my hand where my wound was just healing from our Monday altercation. Great. It would go very nicely with the bruise on my forehead, which had taken on a bright red glow overnight. I was going to be a knockout at David's party this evening, despite the makeup I'd used to cover the knot.

I carried the cat, wiggling and hissing, and tried to stuff him in the cage. Somehow he managed to spread-eagle himself across the open door, but I was bigger than he was, and I used brute force to push him inside. I slammed the door and brushed my hands together to signify a job well done. Spot stared out at me in the same way Betty would have done if she'd been taken to an in-stee-tu-tion. I felt shitty, and by this time my head was pounding again.

"Okay," I said to my houseguest. "I have to get to work, so make yourself at home." Nat had put fresh linen on the rollaway this morning. To give her privacy, we'd put up a screen of the Denver skyline that I'd hand painted in a quieter time. Nat had also gone shopping to replenish my depleted stock of food.

"There's stuff to eat in the refrigerator," I told Betty, stopping only to take a couple more pain pills. "I'll be home at five-thirty and then I'm going to a party. If my date arrives before I get home, just let him in. His name is David, and he won't bite, scratch, or walk all over you."

CHAPTER 23

Spot and I arrived at work at noon. The old hands among my crew, namely Mack and Hernando Lopez, were delighted to see the cat. He gave them an aloof look as he sauntered off to explore the place. I wondered if I'd ever find him again. At this point I wasn't sure I cared.

Mack had agreed to come in early when I called him last night to tell him what had happened. In fact he'd wanted to come over right then and baby-sit me. I shushed Nat into silence so Mack wouldn't know he was there and said all I needed was a full night's sleep. It would have been, too, if Nat hadn't kept waking me to check that I was still conscious.

The more I'd thought about it on the way to work, the more uneasy I felt about leaving Betty alone all evening. I'd brought her home to protect her, and here I was going out to a party and leaving her by herself.

I went over to Mack and gave him my most pitiful smile. "Do you suppose you could do me a favor?"

"Sure, I'll be glad to."

I'd figured he would be nice because of my injuries.

"Do you suppose you could come over tonight and keep Betty company? I'm going to a party."

"Baby-sit Betty?" His voice boomed around the plant even more than usual. "I told you not to take her home."

I knew I should have asked Nat. At least he approved of my houseguest, but I figured Betty would be more comfortable with Mack. She already knew him.

Bribery seemed the only form of persuasion that might work. "I'll come in and tend the boiler all next week," I said.

"Baby-sit a bag lady?" He sounded so irritated, I knew he was going to be perfect in his role in *Twelve Angry Men*. At least if he was an especially grouchy juror.

"I'll buy twenty-five tickets to your play and give them out to customers," I added, even though I didn't approve of an all-male cast of jurors. "It starts next week, doesn't it?"

He was weakening. "Wednesday," he said, "and unfortunately we don't have a rehearsal tonight, but the cast is meeting for an early dinner. What time is this big date of yours?"

"Six-thirty."

"I can't get there till seven."

"That's fine. I'll tell Betty to be expecting you."

I hurried to the call office before he had a chance to change his mind. My front-end people had everything under control on the counter.

"I have to go buy a dress for a party," I said to Julia. "I'll be back in an hour."

"What did you do, run into a door?" she asked.

"I'll tell you later," I said, heading back to my office to get my wrinkled trench coat.

Lucille was inspecting and bagging clothes, and she had more serious concerns than my head injury.

"You're not going to bring that cat back here, are you?" she asked as I passed the work station where Spot had established himself near her feet. "I never did like it when Chet had the cat here."

It wasn't that she had a phobia the way Betty did. She just didn't like the hairs. Sensing that, Spot had found her and was preparing to shed a few as we spoke.

"I was always finding cat hairs on the clothes," she said. "They floated around in the air like germs."

I'd heard her complaint before, which was one of the reasons I moved Spot home in the first place. Lucille had constantly shown me the roller that we ran over the finished clothes just before we bagged them. "See," she'd say. "Those are cat hairs."

"It's just for a few days," I promised, and took off quickly before Spot jumped on her table and really aggravated her.

As I walked the short distance to the stores in Cherry Creek North, I pulled the collar of my trench coat up around my neck to try to block out the cold. Last night I'd felt like a private eye in the trench coat; today I felt like someone who should be spending her money on some heavy outerwear, not a party dress.

Fabergé Dress Salon where Maggie worked was several blocks west on Second Avenue, surrounded by other high-priced specialty stores and boutique-type shops. With Christmas now only a couple of weeks away, the area was jammed with both cars and foot traffic. I was glad I didn't have to find a place to park.

I hoped Maggie would be at the store, but if she wasn't, maybe I could find out something about her from one of the other salespeople. So what if it took my yearly budget for food to buy the dress there? It ought to make the saleslady more talkative.

Surprisingly no one was in the store when I arrived, but I must have set off an alarm in back, because I heard someone approaching almost immediately.

"Mandy," a voice said as I was trying to look for price tags on the dresses. There weren't any. It was a bad sign, kind of like seeing lobster advertised at "market price" on the menu in an expensive restaurant.

I swung around. It was Maggie, looking like a model right out of *Vogue*. "Hi, there," I said, yanking off the old trench coat so I'd be halfway presentable. "I'm looking for a dress."

She touched the coral fabric of my knubby wool suit. "Is that a Donna Karan?"

"Yes," I said, talking designer labels the way we salesladies, country-club members, and dry cleaners do. I'd deliberately chosen to wear the suit today so I wouldn't feel quite so out of place in the salon, and I thought it was nice of Maggie not to mention that the suit was several years out of style and clashed with the fire-red welt on my forehead.

"I need an after-five dress for a party I'm going to tonight," I said. "What do you suggest?"

"What kind of party?"

"It's an office Christmas party at some hotel." I paused. "I'm going with David Withers."

She gave me a blank look.

"You probably know him," I continued. "He was in the cleaners the other morning when you were there."

"Oh, yes, was he the man in the dress shoes and the leisure wear?" she asked.

I could tell by the way she said it that she didn't approve. The correct accessories were everything to people who believe in the coordinated look.

"Yes, that was David," I admitted.

Actually I'd been hoping she'd say something about Betty and the bloody suit so she'd think the topic was her idea. She didn't, apparently too upset by David's lack of fashion finesse.

"It was the day when Betty the Bag Lady came in," I said.

She took the bait at last. "I've been reading about that. It was terrible about the murder."

"Did you know Harrison Van Dyke?"

"No, but his wife shops with us."

Like she was going to tell me if she was having a torrid affair with him. What did I expect?

"You mean her husband never came in with her?"

"No, in fact she usually came in with her friend, Alicia Adamson."

It was my turn to look blank.

She smiled at me as if this was some sort of inside joke. "You know, Mrs. Adamson, the woman who was in the cleaners Monday morning and became so upset by the bag lady that she left?"

"Oh." I suddenly got the punch line, but not simply the one she found amusing.

Here was another lead to pursue. Maybe Mrs. Adamson had mentioned to her good friend, Sybil Van Dyke, how offended she'd been with the bag lady who'd found a suit in a trash can. Mrs. Van could have thought that her consort in crime, whoever he was, had been seen by the bag lady and sicced him on poor Betty's trail. Except that I'd had Eric Jenkins tagged as her accomplice, and he was dead.

"Did you hear about one of the junior partners in the firm?" I asked Maggie.

She shook her head.

"Eric Jenkins?"

"No, I don't think I know him."

"He was killed last night too."

She put her hand to her mouth to hide a slight gasp. "Oh, dear, there's so much crime these days that I hate to be out after dark. My husband always insists on coming to get me when I work late. You know, the streets are so scary when you have to go to your car at night."

So she had a husband? A protective husband who came to get her after work? Was he also jealous? Did this eliminate her as a suspect or simply add her husband to the list? Now I had two other people to consider, including Mrs. Adamson. I just needed some quality quiet time to think about it.

"Now, let's see what we can do for you about that dress you wanted," Maggie said.

Too bad. Now that I'd talked to her, I was ready to leave. Get myself over to one of the department stores that carried price tags on their clothes.

"I think red and green both would look wonderful with your dark hair," she said, ever mindful of the Christmas theme. "I know those are two of my best colors, and I think I have just the thing for you."

She came out with one of those beaded-sequined numbers that weighed a ton and would be like wearing a suit of armor. I declined, saying that such gowns with their "spot clean only" care labels were a curse to dry cleaners, and I couldn't in good conscience wear one.

She left and returned with a rose-colored silk dress. It had a scoop neckline and a low back. I loved it.

"How much?" I asked hopefully.

"Twelve hundred," she said, "and a real steal at the price."

I could agree with that. Even a burglar would be happy with a twelve-hundred-dollar haul.

Maybe it wouldn't fit, and of course I didn't have time for alterations. That would get me off the hook. Unfortunately the dress fit like it was molded to my body. I could see the dollar signs floating over Maggie's head, and I knew I had to get out of this.

"You know," I said, sounding like my teenage employee, Ann Marie, "what with Christmas shopping and all, I'm a little short this month. . . ." My nose began to itch as if I was Cyrano de Bergerac with a head cold. I guess it was because I hadn't even started a Christmas list. The part about being short of cash was true though—about a thousand dollars short.

"You know," I repeated, "I have a perfectly good basic-black dress at home. Maybe I should just accessorize. I love that scarf on the mannequin by the door. I couldn't help noticing it as I came in."

Actually I hadn't really paid much attention to it. When Maggie brought it to me, I saw that it looked like an abstract painting with a swirl of Christmas colors on it. Frankly I liked some of my own work much better. Maybe I should become an artist for designer scarves. When Maggie said it cost eighty-five dollars, I knew I'd missed my calling.

I gulped and said I'd take it. I figured it was the cheapest thing in the salon—except for me. I bought it and started to make my escape, trying to convince myself that I'd gotten a bargain. Never mind that I was going to look as if I belonged on the wall of some art gallery down the street.

I tried to look at it as if I'd gotten eighty-five dollars' worth of information out of the conversation. If Maggie had been a bartender, I might have had to pay that much money just to get her to talk. This way I also had a scarf.

Well, the information and the scarf hadn't really been worth eighty-five dollars. Not yet. "Oh, by the way," I said, "you wouldn't happen to have Mrs. Adamson's phone number, would you?"

"I'm sorry, Mandy. We can't give out that information."

"It's just—well, I'd like to call and apologize for any embarrassment she may have suffered. It would mean a lot to me."

Maggie hesitated. "Oh, all right. I'll be right back."

She went in the back room and returned with the phone number on a piece of paper. "Please don't tell her I gave it to you."

"You can count on me, Maggie." I paused. "We sound like twins, don't we—Maggie and Mandy? My name's actually Amanda. Is Maggie short for something—Margaret perhaps?"

"No, I wish it were. My given name is Magdalena. I hated it when I was growing up."

After I left, there was something about the conversation

that nagged at me—Magdalena or no. I didn't think it was what I'd learned about Mrs. Adamson or the fact that Maggie might have a jealous husband. Maybe it was that a scarf, knotted around my neck, would give Betty another choke hold if she became dissatisfied with our living arrangements.

CHAPTER 24

It was approaching zero hour as far as my big dress-up date was concerned. I had to go home and press my dress, plus shower and reapply the makeup to my bruised forehead, but I still had one thing I wanted to do before I left work.

I went to my office and dialed the phone.

"Mrs. Adamson, please," I said when a woman answered.

"This is she." I would have known it was, just by her grammatically correct form of speech.

"This is Amanda Dyer of Dyer's Cleaners. I was calling to apologize for any inconvenience you may have suffered Monday morning when you came into our store."

"Hmmph," she said.

My nose began to itch at the lie. Actually I was still amused by Betty's banter that morning. It must be the bohemian part of me that makes me feel that way when snobbish folks get their comeuppance.

"I'm really sorry, and we'd like to extend a complimentary offer to you to try our services again," I said. "I know you'll find the care we give your clothes to be the best in town."

"Free?" she asked. "As much as I want to bring in?"

"Yes." I nearly choked on the word. I had a feeling this was going to cost me big-time.

"Well, one of my friends did recommend you. . . ."

"Oh, incidentally, I understand you're a friend of Mrs. Van Dyke, and I did want to ask a personal favor."

"What?" she asked suspiciously.

"I would be ever so grateful if you wouldn't say anything to her about the incident. You know, she's one of our most valued customers, and the suit that the homeless woman brought into the store may have figured in the death of Mrs. Van Dyke's husband."

"I know. Poor Sybil."

"I was so afraid you might have mentioned it to her before you found out about her husband."

"Certainly not." Mrs. Adamson sniffed, and I had a gut feeling from the way she said it that she was telling the truth. It would have been too embarrassing for her to recount her encounter with Betty to anyone.

I tried to sound relieved, but to tell the truth, I'd been hoping she'd inadvertently passed the information along to the Van Dyke household that Betty had brought in the bloody suit.

"That's a great relief, Mrs. Adamson," I said, "and I'll give your clothes my personal attention when you come in."

I was sweating when I hung up. God, it was hard being gracious sometimes. I glanced at my watch. I should have been home by now. Maybe I'd have to skip the shower. Nope, I didn't think so.

I went to grab my trench coat, but Spot was lying on it.

He looked as if he were waiting to go home, too, now that he'd found someone there to antagonize.

"Sorry, Spot." I pulled the trench coat gently out from under him.

He growled at me.

I looked at the trench coat covered with cat hairs and realized it was the only thing I had to wear over my dress tonight. I was going to look like Columbo in drag.

I dug through the to-do pile on the top of my desk, looking for my newly purchased scarf. Mustn't forget that. As soon as I found it, I was out of here.

I'd already told my counter crew that I was leaving, and fortunately Mack had been gone when I returned from my shopping spree, so I didn't have to worry about his questions. I had the back door open when I heard Sarah yell at me.

"I'm glad I caught you," she said. "There's a policeman up front, and he says he has to speak to you."

Talk about bad timing. Now that I had a previous engagement, I supposed Foster was going to ask me out again.

I turned around and headed to the call office.

I didn't see him when I arrived. "Where's Detective Foster?" I asked.

A strange man flashed his badge at me. "I'm Detective Cahill," he said, "and I'm working on the case with Stan."

"Oh." I was disappointed despite my tight schedule. In fact if I'd had a chance to think about it earlier, I'd have been disappointed that he didn't at least call.

"I wanted to review this report with you that we got from the Aurora PD."

"I'm running late. Could we do it tomorrow?"

"It'll just take a few minutes."

I took him inside the door to the plant and asked if we could talk at Lucille's mark-in table.

He seemed agreeable, and he pulled out a notebook and pen. After he confirmed everything I'd already told Detective Lucero, he said I was free to leave. I couldn't do it. Not without telling him about Nat's and my idea that the killer could have found out about Betty right here at the cleaners. Detective Cahill was about as excited at the theory as Foster had been with the hair samples Wednesday night. Unfortunately it also meant I would no longer have an excuse to call Foster about it.

But always the good citizen, I gave Cahill a list of the customers who'd been in the store Monday morning and their possible connections to the case. I had a feeling Mrs. Adamson would never come into the cleaners again once I'd given the cops her name. Maybe it was just as well after my offer for the complimentary cleaning.

When I mentioned David, I looked at my watch. If I left right now, I might get home with fifteen minutes to spare before he arrived. Cahill saw me checking the time. He must have been looking for an excuse to leave. He said he didn't want to detain me any longer, thanked me for my help, and left.

I hurried to the back door, where Spot sat back on his haunches waiting for me. He meowed as if to say, "Hey, you're not bustin' out of here without me." No, it was more of a feed-me cry. I could tell the difference.

"Oh, damn. You're probably hungry, aren't you? Or you need a litter box."

There was no time to go for kitty litter or carryout cat food. The only thing for it was to take Spot home whether Betty liked it or not. I could always stick Spot in the closet until tomorrow morning. I thought of my own captivity in the closet and cringed. Well, we'd think of something.

I whisked him up in my arms. He was so surprised, he didn't even hiss or growl as I stuck him in the cat carrier.

David was due at my apartment in twenty-five minutes. Maybe I could catch him before he left. Tell him I'd be a half hour late. I booted up the computer, checked his home phone number, and dialed it. No answer. His address indicated that he lived in South Denver, out by the Denver Tech Center. With his compulsion for punctuality he'd probably be at my door precisely at six-thirty. I hated not being ready when he arrived. I'd already made him wait the other time we went to dinner.

I called Betty, and for a minute I was afraid she wasn't going to pick up.

"Thank God you're there," I said.

"Where'd you expect me to be?" I could tell she was a little perturbed. She didn't even call me Princess. That's what I got for checking on her every hour throughout the afternoon.

"My date hasn't arrived, has he?"

"No."

"Good. Can you iron?"

"Huh?"

"Can you iron clothes?"

"Can the queen curtsy?"

Oh, good, her sense of humor was back, and I took it as a yes. A little like "Is the pope Catholic?"

"Would you do me a big favor?" I didn't wait for her to answer. "There's this black dress hanging in my closet. I need to wear it tonight, but it's wrinkled. Could you iron it for me? The ironing board is right inside the closet door, and the iron is under the kitchen sink."

For a minute I thought she was going to refuse, but all she said was "Okay. Bye" and hung up on me.

Come to think of it, could the queen curtsy? I wasn't sure. Maybe only the queen's subjects had to learn how. And maybe Betty couldn't iron at all. Still, it was what I deserved. Me, the dry cleaner with all the equipment for a perfect press, entrusting my only good dress to a bag lady.

I hauled Spot out the back door. Betty probably wasn't going to be happy to see the cat, but then I might not be happy with the way she ironed.

It had finally started to snow, after threatening since last night. I started the van and skidded on a patch of ice as I drove out of the parking lot. That's all I needed was to be all dressed up in three-inch heels in a blinding snowstorm. Maybe I could borrow Betty's combat boots. I tried to remember if I'd had that broken heel replaced on my only pair of black pumps. Now was a fine time to think about shoes.

Shoes? Suddenly I remembered what Maggie had said that had gnawed at the back of my mind all afternoon. David in his dress shoes and his leisure wear. In Kmart English, that meant a jogging suit. A tan jogging suit! Could that translate to Sahara Sunset or Sand Dune?

Oh, God, don't even think about it. I had to stop for a red light at Speer Boulevard and Downing, but I'd have run it if a double stack of cars hadn't been in the lanes ahead of me.

I yanked out my sketch pad from my purse and switched on the overhead light so I could take a look at the sketches I'd made of Betty's assailant the other day at the hospital. I'd sketched a ski-masked guy in a dark jacket and light pants, and I'd darkened in the shoes as if they were expensive footwear.

No, no, no. It couldn't be. Not David? Not the guy with the shoes with the tassels on them that Betty had talked about. I banged my hand on the steering wheel in frustration at the red light going off in my head.

The light turned green, but I could hardly see it because the snow was getting heavier now. I stepped on the accelerator even before the driver started up ahead of me. I nearly rear-ended him, and I turned right on Downing just so he'd be out of my way.

I hadn't figured it out, but it was getting scarier all the time. I began to size up David against the profile I'd compiled for the owner of the bloody suit. About five-eight or five-nine, light brown or blond hair. David, the tan man with his light brown hair and slightly off-kilter clothes sense. Someone who had gained weight since he bought the suit. That fit David, which was why I'd been pleased that he'd finally started going to the gym.

The only reason I'd assumed he was working out was because of the jogging suit. I'd even inquired if the gym was in the neighborhood, but when I'd asked him about it, he'd told me he went to a gym over on the west side of town, in Lakewood. I'd just seen his address and it was south, not west.

And there was the cigarette burn in the suit. David had been a smoker. He'd told me his ex-wife had always wanted him to quit. What was her name? I tried to remember it.

Pat? Penny? No, Peg.

"Peg," I yelled the name like a curse. Wasn't that sometimes used as a nickname for Margaret? I knew it was, and I could have throttled myself for not thinking of it sooner. I slammed down the sketch pad on Spot's cage. The poor cat hissed.

"I'm sorry, fella," I said, and pressed down on the accelerator as I went through a yellow light at Eighth Avenue. I was going too fast for the conditions, but I didn't care. I wanted a policeman to pull me over. Then I could get him to call for help and provide me with an escort so I could get home before David arrived. There was never a cop around when you needed one.

I thought about stopping at a pay phone. Tell the dispatcher to send someone to my apartment before there was another murder. But I was afraid it would take too long to find a phone.

I took a left at Thirteenth, a one-way street heading toward downtown and my apartment. "I should have put a phone in the van," I said aloud, as if Spot cared.

Why hadn't I done it when I started the business route? I'd known I should get a car phone to communicate with my driver when he was running the route, but I'd never figured I'd need it to call the police.

The best thing to do under the circumstances was get home before David showed up and discovered Betty, the woman he'd been trying to kill since Monday. I'd tell her to hide in the bathroom, then call 911 and act as if nothing was wrong when David arrived. Just stall him until the police got there.

"Yeah, that should work," I mumbled, checking the time. Six-eighteen and counting.

I ran a red light, but had to slow down for a car that was creeping along through the snow. The roads were so slippery now that I couldn't get any traction as I tried to speed up again. Why had my mind decided to kick into gear when the damned van wouldn't move?

David had even told me Eric was his wife's attorney in their divorce proceedings. He'd seemed angry and said his wife and Eric had been having an affair on the side. Actually "an orgy" is what he said. I'd thought at the time that David could have been a suspect if Eric had been the murder victim. Now Eric was, and didn't an "orgy" convey more than one partner? A ménage à trois with Harrison Van Dyke? And David had said I kind of reminded him of his ex-wife. I had curly dark hair, even though it wasn't as long or kinky as the hairs I'd found on Van Dyke's sweaters.

The irony was that I'd asked David about Eric because I'd noticed them exchanging greetings outside the cleaners Monday morning. I'd been asking the wrong guy for information. I bet Eric had remembered the jogging suit David had worn that morning, the one that looked exactly like his. He could have realized it was his missing outfit from the cleaning closet.

I couldn't even guess as to how David figured out Eric was on to him.

I checked my watch again. Six twenty-two. Good. Eight minutes to spare. I was approaching my street, and I slid around the corner to my apartment. No parking places in front. I double-parked, but I grabbed the cat carrier because I didn't want Spot to freeze to death shut up in the van during a blizzard.

"Sorry—" I was really losing it, apologizing to a cat all the time. I yanked him out of the van and bounced him up the sidewalk to the front door. My headache was back big-time, but I took the steps to my apartment two at a time. All I needed was a couple of minutes to stuff Betty away someplace while I dialed 911 and waited for the police. Then I'd take some pain pills.

When I reached the door, I banged on it. "Open up, Betty. Hurry." I knocked again, but finally I had to set the cat carrier down to search out the apartment key on the ring in my hand.

Before I got the key in the lock, the door opened.

"David," I said. "What a surprise. You're early."

CHAPTER 25

"Come on in and join the party," David said, holding the door for me.

Betty didn't say anything. She was standing a few feet from the end of the ironing board, and I could see my black dress, all neatly pressed and hung on a hanger over the screen behind her.

I was shaking so hard, I was sure David would notice.

"Brrr," I said, hoping that would explain my tremors. "It's cold out there."

I dragged the cat carrier inside and bent down to let Spot out of his cage. The cat, ignoring all my mental pleas to attack, stalked over to his food dish. As long as I was already on the floor, I took a peek at David's shoes.

My heart froze. He was wearing the shoes with the tassels on them, just like the ones Betty had described. Okay, you have to be nonchalant, I told myself. Act as if nothing's wrong, and get David out of here as fast as possible.

I glanced over at Betty as I got up. She was staring down

at the shoes like a person with a foot fetish. Talk about a dead giveaway.

While I tried to think of what to do, I took off my coat and put it on the coatrack by the door. "I'll be ready in just a minute," I said as I started to remove my suit jacket. If I could just get him to the party, I could always call 911 from there.

"I'm not in any rush," he said. "Betty seems to think she's seen me before, and we were trying to figure out where."

Oh, damn, he knew who she was, even without the bag. I forgot about taking off the jacket; I needed to get him out of here *Now*. "Well, David works down by Cherry Creek, so you probably *have* seen him, Betty."

She gave me a how-dumb-can-you-be look and kind of twitched her head a couple of times in the direction of the shoes.

I refused to look at his feet, but I noticed he was wearing a charcoal-gray suit that went nicely with the tasseled shoes. This was no time for him to get coordinated. Why couldn't he have worn a pair of Nikes or something equally inappropriate that Betty wouldn't have recognized?

If I couldn't get David out, I at least needed to remove Betty from the room. "Will you take Spot into the bathroom, Betty, and get him some water? There's a dish right by the litter box, and he hasn't had anything to drink all day."

"I don't think so," David said as Betty started to leave.

"What are you talking about?" I asked. He pointed to a bowl by the empty food dish. "There's water right there, and besides, Betty knows who I am."

"Of course she knows who you are. I told her you'd be stopping by because we were going to a Christmas party."

How could I have done this to Betty? Just open the door and let him in, I'd said, he won't bite, scratch, or walk all over you. I'd failed to mention that he might kill her.

"She saw me in the cleaners," David said. "I knew she recognized me—the way she kept looking everyplace but at me."

"Never seen you before in my life, mister," Betty chimed in with her first words of the evening.

"Oh, yeah, you did," David said. "When I threw away the suit."

Damn, damn. Now he'd admitted it, and I supposed there was no way of pretending we didn't know what he was talking about.

"Betty and I were just getting ready to take a little walk," he continued. "Too bad you got here when you did."

"How do you plan to get rid of both of us, David?" After all, I thought, how many people carry weapons around with them when they're going to a Christmas party? Dumb me.

"With this." He whipped a gun out of his pants pocket as if it were our invitation to the ball. "I've taken to carrying it in my glove compartment after crime started getting so bad in the neighborhood."

"Oh." I sounded like one of Spot's old squeaky toys.

He pointed the gun at me. "Lucky I called on my car phone to tell you I was on the way. Betty said the 'princess' wasn't here yet. I knew it was her because I heard her call you that Monday morning."

Betty and her stupid nickname.

"Get over there." He waved the gun to indicate I should move away from the door.

I joined Betty near the ironing board. She had turned at an angle to David, and now the pupils of her eyes began to dance from the ironing board to me and back again as if she were trying to tell me something.

Okay, sure, Betty, you did a nice job on the dress. If we ever get out of this situation, maybe I'll hire you to operate one of the shirt presses at work.

I needed to figure out how to buy some time, but it was hard to do with all Betty's eye movements and head jerks. Maybe I could keep David talking for half an hour until Mack showed up to stay with Betty. Mack had played the part of a heavyweight boxer in *The Great White Hope*, after all.

"Betty never saw anyone get rid of the suit, David," I said.

She threw up her arms as if she couldn't believe I was going to continue this conversation.

David edged toward us. For a second I thought he was going to step on Spot's tail, and I fantasized that Spot and I could both go for him simultaneously. Instead the cat swished his tail out of the way and continued to sit at attention by the empty dish.

"So how'd Betty know it was me?" David demanded. "I could tell she recognized me the moment I walked in here tonight."

"It was the shoes, David," I said. "She saw them when you attacked her down at the plant."

David glanced down at the shoes, but not for long enough that I could throw myself at his feet and try to wrestle him to the floor.

"I bet they're the ones you were wearing when you were in the cleaners Monday morning," I said. "Don't you know you aren't supposed to wear the same shoes every day? They're bad for your feet."

Betty rolled her eyes as if I'd gone completely daft, talking podiatry.

"Forget about my feet," David yelled, waving the gun wildly. "I'm going to have to kill you. You know that, don't you?"

Spot let out a plaintive meow. If humans weren't going to respond to his rigid body language, he'd have to try his verbal skills.

"At least you owe us some explanation of why you're doing this," I said. "Van Dyke was having an affair with your ex-wife, Margaret, wasn't he?"

He nodded, tears coming to his eyes. "She left town after the divorce, but she came back. I thought maybe we could patch things up, but she started playing around with him again. They were shacked up in that big fancy office of his all night."

"So you waited outside for her to leave?"

"No, I followed them in before the door closed, just like I told you someone could have done." His eyes took on a glazed look. "I heard them making noises like animals."

As if on cue, Spot let out another meow.

"It was awful," David said, covering an ear with one hand but still pointing the gun at us with the other. "I waited until she left. All I wanted to do was talk to him, tell him to leave her alone, but he wouldn't listen." He shuddered at the memory.

"Oh, sure, like anyone's going to believe that this wasn't premeditated," I said. "You take a knife with you, and you wear—what?—your wedding suit to the office as if it were some kind of ritualistic killing."

I was just rambling, but maybe I'd hit a nerve.

"Shut up, you slut," David screamed.

"What did you do—steal the plastic bag with her hair in it too?" It was a dumb question, but he closed his eyes as if that would shut out my voice. I made a movement toward him, but he opened his eyes quickly and pointed the gun at my chest.

I had to keep him talking, but Betty was so distracting that I couldn't think. She continued to do jerky little movements with her head toward the ironing board. I finally saw what she was trying to show me. Maybe. The iron was still plugged in and hot as a pistol, so to speak. I didn't know what to do about it, but it was the only weapon around. I took a step toward it.

David saw the movement. "Stand back over there by Betty."

I returned to my original position. Spot must have thought I'd finally decided to feed him. He began to meow big-time.

"Will you make that damned cat stop meowing," David said.

"Be quiet, Spot," I yelled. Maybe the neighbors would hear me and wonder what was going on, but no one clattered up the stairs to the rescue. "So why'd you steal Eric's jogging suit from our cleaning closet?"

He shrugged. "I was just trying to find something to wear—a coat, a janitor's uniform, anything to cover up the blood. And then I found those dirty clothes in the bags. I went through them until I found something that would fit. I didn't know it was Eric's jogging suit. . . ." His voice trailed off.

"But seeing the Dyer's Cleaners bags must have given

you the idea to come to the cleaners to get some of your own clothes," I said. "Then you wouldn't have to go all the way home to change for work. Right, David?"

He looked surprised. "Right. I didn't know Betty was going to bring in the suit. I didn't think anyone had seen me throw it away, but she sounded like she knew something."

"I didn't see nuttin'." Betty shook her head as if it had come unhinged from her neck.

I took a look at my watch. Only five minutes had gone by since I got home. I'd never make it until Mack arrived, but I had to try. "And of course you didn't know you'd run into Eric right outside the cleaners, did you?"

"I didn't even know it was his stupid outfit until he called Peg and asked her about it. Little did he know that we were back talking again." David stopped and took a deep breath. "Eric deserved to die too. He was the one who turned Peg on to all that sick sex."

"But we don't deserve to die, David. How are you going to rationalize shooting us?"

David seemed to waver for the first time. "But you *know*," he said. "I was afraid you knew all along. That's why I had to keep taking you out—to find out what you knew. I didn't want to have to hurt you."

"You broke into the cleaners Monday night, didn't you?"

"I called you to make sure you were home," he said, defending his action. "You answered the phone."

"So you were the heavy breather who didn't say anything," I said.

"I thought it was safe to break into the cleaners with you at home. It was a cinch to break out that window you never bothered to hook up to the alarm system. Who knew you were going to show up down there? I needed to find the suit."

"It wasn't there. I turned it over to the police."

"I know that now." David stomped his feet, making the tassels dance. "I don't want to talk about it anymore."

Spot didn't like the sudden noise. He cut a wide swath around David, came over to Betty, and plopped down in front of her.

"I have to get everything cleaned up," David said as if he were the dry cleaner. "You're the last loose end, and then I think I can get Peg back. She needs me now because I'm her alibi for the time Van Dyke was killed. Can you fancy that? She didn't even know I needed an alibi."

"But we haven't done anything to you," I said. "You can't shoot two innocent people."

"Oh, yes, I can. I'll show you." He pointed the gun at Spot. "I'll kill the cat."

Betty let out a gasp. "No, you don't." She snatched Spot from the floor and held him to her chest.

For God's sake, now he'd shoot them both with one bullet. I lunged for the ironing board. David was right behind me.

He grabbed me around the neck and put the gun to my head, but my hand was already around the handle of the iron. I reached back and slammed it into his cheek.

He let out a shriek and put the hand with the gun in it to his face, the barrel pointed to the ceiling. I twisted out of his grasp and drove the iron into his knuckles. The gun flew out of his hand, and we both dove for it. One of the legs of my panty hose popped open at the knee as I landed on top of him. I was still holding the iron, and I jammed it against his suit jacket as if I were going to give it a quick press.

"God damn you," he screamed, twisting in pain under my body.

A seam in my jacket ripped as I struggled to stay on top of him, but I managed to keep the iron burrowed into his back with my right hand. With my other one, I stretched out and tried to get the gun. I couldn't reach it. The best I could do was give it a shove across the floor to Betty.

She stared at it the way she'd stared at the shoes.

"Get the damned gun, Betty," I yelled.

That brought her out of her trance. She dropped Spot and grabbed the gun. The cat took off as if the devil were on his tail.

And suddenly Betty the Bag Lady turned into Ma Barker.

"Freeze, you son of a bitch," she said, pointing the gun at David's head.

CHAPTER 26

Actually Betty was pointing the gun at my head, too, since I was still on top of David. I took a lesson from Spot and got out of the line of fire as fast as I could.

I scrambled to Betty's side where I had to put down the iron to pry the gun out of her hand. She didn't want to let go.

"I'll take it from here," I said.

Somehow I felt more comfortable holding the gun myself, even though my hand started to shake as soon as I grabbed it. I'd been fine with the iron, but for a minute I'd been afraid Betty would just shoot David and be done with it.

She kept letting out a stream of cusswords as if the dam had broken. Meanwhile the object of her contempt was curled up on the floor writhing in pain.

"Go call Nine-one-one," I told her.

"That stupid asshole shithead," she said.

"Go call Nine-one-one," I repeated.

She went to the phone reluctantly and punched in the numbers. "What do you want me to tell them—that we got us a dead one here?" she asked.

"Tell them we have Harrison Van Dyke's killer."

She repeated the words into the phone and then turned to me, "What's the address?"

I kept feeding her the lines, and she said them into the phone, fortunately deleting all of her earlier expletives.

"Tell the dispatcher to call Detective Stan Foster," I said.

"You burned me," David whimpered. "I need something for the pain." He started to get up.

I steadied the gun by propping my arms on the kitchen counter. "Don't even think about it, David, I'm warning you."

He lay back down, rolling from side to side like a contortionist with the cramps.

"They want me to stay on the phone," Betty said, putting her hand over the mouthpiece to let me know.

"Well, then, stay on the phone."

"But what do I say?"

"Don't say anything. Just keep the line open."

"Okay, but that seems dumb."

David groaned.

Betty covered up the mouthpiece again. "We ought to shoot the bastard and put him out of his misery."

David quieted down.

"Anyone tries to shoot a cat ought to be shot hisself," Betty continued.

"I thought you didn't like Spot," I said.

"I don't, but I guess he kind of reminds me of me. We're both nothin' but old alley cats, but we ain't hurtin' nobody."

Someone banged on the door a few minutes later. It was great response time, which is one of the advantages of living in a high-crime area. There are always some patrol cars out cruising the neighborhood.

Betty slammed down the phone when she heard the knocking. She went over and sat down in the overstuffed chair where Spot had done his little circling act this morning.

"I thought you were never going to catch on to that iron," she said. "If you don't mind my saying so, Princess, you're a little slow on the uptake."

I went to the door, but I kept the gun aimed at David.

"I'm beginnin' to think livin' on the street is a whole lot safer than livin' with you," she continued.

"Who's there?" I asked.

"It's me, Mack."

Oh, great. *Now* he shows up. It was going to be as bad as having Mom here, but I let him in.

"I'm a little early," he said before he noticed the gun. "What the devil is going on?"

I wiggled the barrel toward David. "He's the owner of the bloody suit."

"Let me have that thing." Mack made a motion to take the gun. There was another bang on the door. "This is the police," someone yelled.

No way was I giving up the gun. Especially to Mack. A big black guy who looks like an aging prizefighter didn't need to be holding a weapon when I greeted the cops.

I dropped the gun to my side and opened the door.

"Are you the one who called?" the cop asked.

"Yes, and we need to make sure Detective Foster knows about this," I said. "He's been looking for the guy over there." I pointed at David with a head nod, careful not to use my trigger finger.

"We'll take the gun now, ma'am," a second cop said.

"It's all yours." I handed it to him slowly so he'd know I didn't have any hard feelings toward him. "We took it away from the killer."

"Christ Almighty, Mandy, you just can't stay out of trouble, can you?" Mack said, his voice booming like a bullhorn.

Once I explained to the men that Mack had just arrived, they made him sit over on the far end of the sofa, away from Betty's chair. Mack kept shaking his head, and Betty muttered to herself.

Foster arrived a few minutes later, all tall and handsome and casual-looking in jeans and a cableknit sweater. By then I'd told the uniformed cops the salient points of David's confession, and the taller of the two went over to David.

"What's going on here?" Foster asked, looking around in surprise.

"We have a suspect in the murder of Harrison Van Dyke," the short cop told him.

"I asked the dispatcher to call you," I said, trying to smooth down my hair, tuck in the tail of my blouse, which was missing a couple of buttons, and adjust my torn jacket all at the same time. "Didn't you get the message?"

Foster shook his head. "I had to go out of town yesterday afternoon. I just got back."

So what was he doing here if it wasn't in response to Betty's call? I liked a few of the ideas that came to mind, but I decided this wouldn't be an appropriate time to ask.

He explained anyway. "I just finished talking to Detective Cahill, and I wanted to ask you a few questions about one of your customers. Why don't you fill me in on what's going on here?"

Okay, so this wasn't a social visit, but I started to answer until I realized he'd turned to the cop. The man repeated what I'd just said to them, and I interrupted only once to point to the couch. "My friend, McKenzie Rivers, wasn't here when it happened, but Betty was a witness."

She had clammed up completely and was staring straight ahead. I guess she'd decided to keep a low profile, just like Spot, who'd disappeared the minute Betty let go of him.

By then several other patrolmen had arrived, and the first cop on the scene turned to them.

Foster looked over to where David had already been handcuffed. "He's the guy who was in the cleaners the other night,"

I nodded. "It would have helped if you'd told me Van Dyke's girlfriend was David Withers's ex-wife."

Foster frowned at me. "Cahill's the one who interviewed him, and once you told him that Withers was in the cleaners Monday morning, we've been out looking for him." He paused. "Incidentally that's the way it's supposed to work. You tell us what you know, not the other way around."

"Okay," I said. "But you already know what happened. David killed Van Dyke and Eric Jenkins, and he tried to kill Betty. He admitted everything."

Betty nodded and pointed to his fancy footwear. "I told you he had funny shoes."

Foster frowned at us. "Go over and sit down," he said. "We'll take you to headquarters in a minute to make a statement, but for the time being, don't talk to each other."

I sat by Mack. He looked as if he had plenty to say to me, but Betty still wasn't in a real talkative mood. She moved her lips occasionally, probably mouthing silent obscenities, which was okay with me. I felt like muttering a few nasty things about David myself. After all, he'd only been asking me out to find out what I knew.

Two of the cops had him on his feet. "He's got a burn on his face," one of them said.

Sure, I thought, and I've got a run in my panty hose, a tear in my best suit jacket, a bruise on my stomach, and the headache from hell, all because of David. So don't expect any sympathy from me.

"Maybe we'd better take him to Denver General and check him out," the man continued.

Foster nodded. "Later."

"We should have shot him," Betty said.

The uniformed cops moved David toward the door. I thought about telling him that his company damned well better pay my claims, since he was the one who broke into my plant and ruined my customers' clothes. I didn't, but he glared at me anyway.

I got up and went over to Foster. "Before we go, do you mind if I look for my cat? He hasn't had anything to eat all day."

"As a matter of fact neither have I," Foster said in a low voice.

Unspoken suggestions for how we could rectify the situation came to mind, but they would have to wait until later. I moved over to the screen that Nat had set up in front of the rollaway bed that morning. As I went by, I couldn't help noticing the dress Betty had ironed for me. She really had done a good job.

"The dress looks great," I told her.

"You didn't do so bad on the guy's face neither," she said. "Both of them were pretty wrinkled." She chuckled.

Maybe she actually would like to come to work at the

cleaners. She would certainly liven up the place. I'd have to give it some thought when I had the time.

Right now I needed to find Spot. The last I'd seen of him was when he went streaking around behind the screen. I was afraid he'd gotten out in all the confusion, but thankfully he was hunched up on the rollaway, glowering at me as if he were saying a few expletives of his own.

I wanted to sit down out of sight of everyone and cuddle him or cry into his fur, just from the relief that the whole ordeal was over, but I knew Spot would be offended. Instead I raised my arms in a close-fisted gesture above my head. "Allll right," I said. "We did it."

Spot looked less than impressed.

"Okay, just stay where you are," I said. "I'll go get you some food."

All of sudden there was more banging at the front door.

"Hey, you can't come in here," someone said.

"Sure I can. I live here."

I recognized Nat's voice. He would use any ruse he could to get a story, and I'd gladly have wrung his neck if there hadn't been entirely too much violence already tonight.

"What are you doing here, Wilcox?" That was Foster.

"Where's Mandy? Is she all right?" Nat had barged into the room by the time I got out from behind the screen.

"I'm okay, Nat," I said.

Foster looked at me and back at Nat. "Are you two . . .?" He seemed as embarrassed as he had Wednesday night at the cleaners when he found out David and I had a dinner date. "Damn right we are," Nat said as he came over and gave me a big hug. "Play along with me, Mandy," he whispered in my ear. "Otherwise they'll throw me out on my butt."

I tried to extricate myself from his grasp.

"I'll owe you big-time," he said.

"You better believe you will." I broke free, but I knew that playing along with Nat might put a serious glitch in any hoped-for relationship with Foster. At the same time, I wasn't sure I wanted to air my laundry, dirty or otherwise, in front of Denver's finest.

Two of the patrolmen escorted Betty and me to police headquarters, where Cahill took our statements separately.

"Good work," he said when the interviews were over. "I'll have someone give you a ride home."

By the time we got back to my apartment, Nat had already filed his story and fed Spot. Then I made him fix sandwiches for Mack and Betty and me. He was going to have to pay and pay and pay.

I took a pain pill and put an ice pack on my head. I couldn't deal with anything more tonight, but the next time I saw Foster, I would set the record straight about Nat and me.

And I knew I would see him again. He might be able to avoid me at the police station or even at the trial, but he'd have to come to Dyer's Cleaners sooner or later.

After all, I had his clothes.

MANDY'S FAVORITE CLEANING TIP

Hair spray will remove ink stains from shirts. (For details, read Chapter 4.)